Many thanks to Mr. and Mrs. Goldenberg, for being such great listeners, and for their advice and encouragement.

—M.L.

For Laurène and Céline, my little family
Thanks:
To Greg the Very Colorful
To Hellen and Bernard, leading the fight to keep memories alive
To Julie, Pôl, and Antoine, as well as the entire team at Le Lombard . . .
Thanks to all of you for your help, your patience, your support, your commitment.
And much more besides. So much more . . .

—L.D.

Thank you to Fred for his support and to Cécile for her help.
—G.S.

For the writing of this book, Loïc Dauvillier received support from France's National Book Center.

First Second

Published by First Second
First Second is an imprint of Roaring Brook Press, a division of Holtzbrinck Publishing Holdings Limited Partnership
175 Fifth Avenue, New York, New York 10010
All rights reserved

Cataloging-in-Publication Data is on file at the Library of Congress

ISBN: 978-1-59643-873-6

First Second books may be purchased for business or promotional use. For information on bulk purchases please contact Macmillan Corporate and Premium Sales Department at (800) 221-7945 x5442 or by email at specialmarkets@macmillan.com.

Originally published in 2012 by Le Lombard under the title *L'Enfant Cachée*

First American edition 2014
Book design by Colleen AF Venable

Printed in China by 1010 Printing International Ltd., North Point, Hong Kong

10 9 8 7

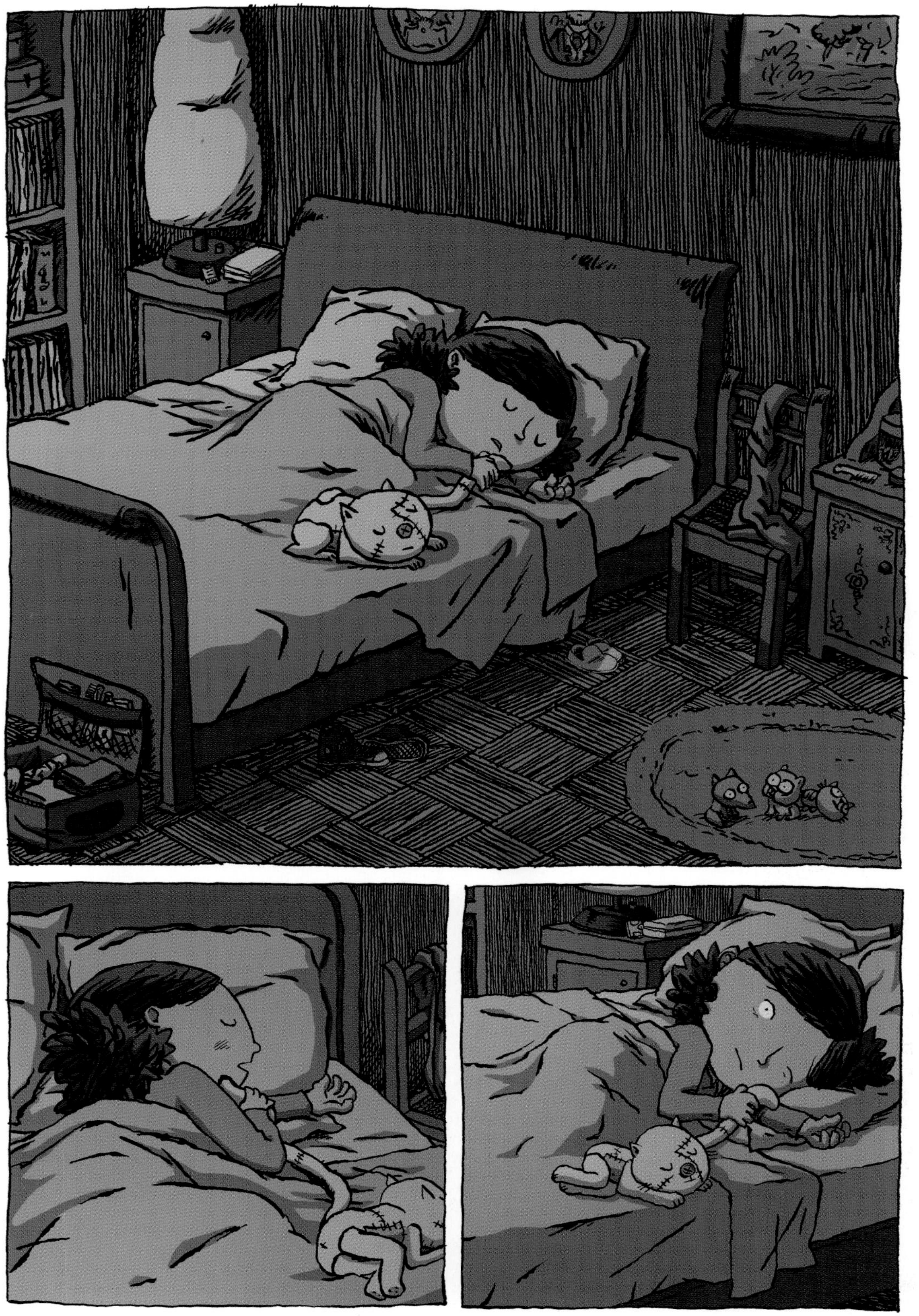

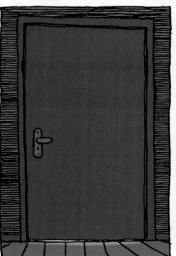

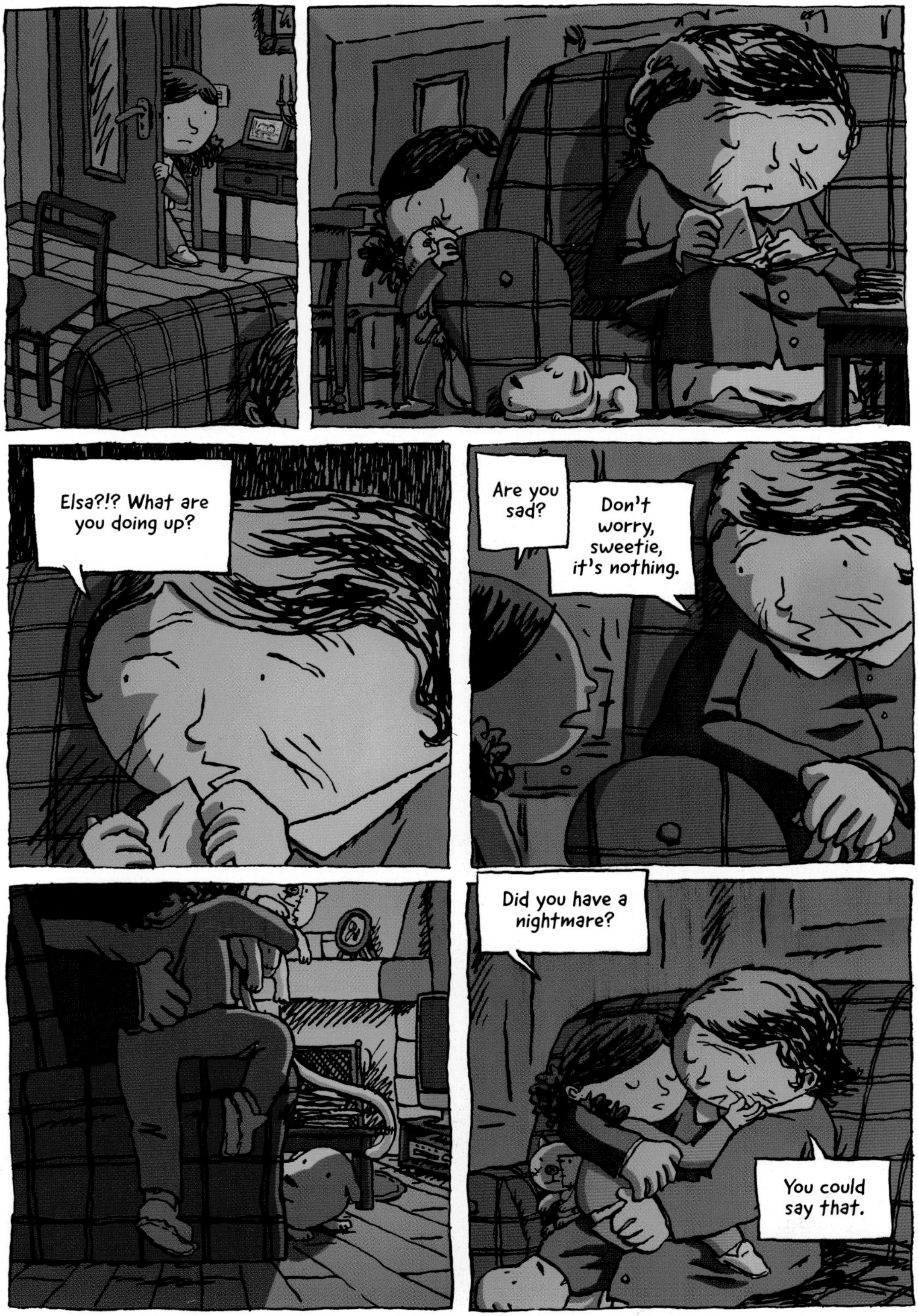
Elsa?!? What are you doing up?
Are you sad?
Don't worry, sweetie, it's nothing.
Did you have a nightmare?
You could say that.

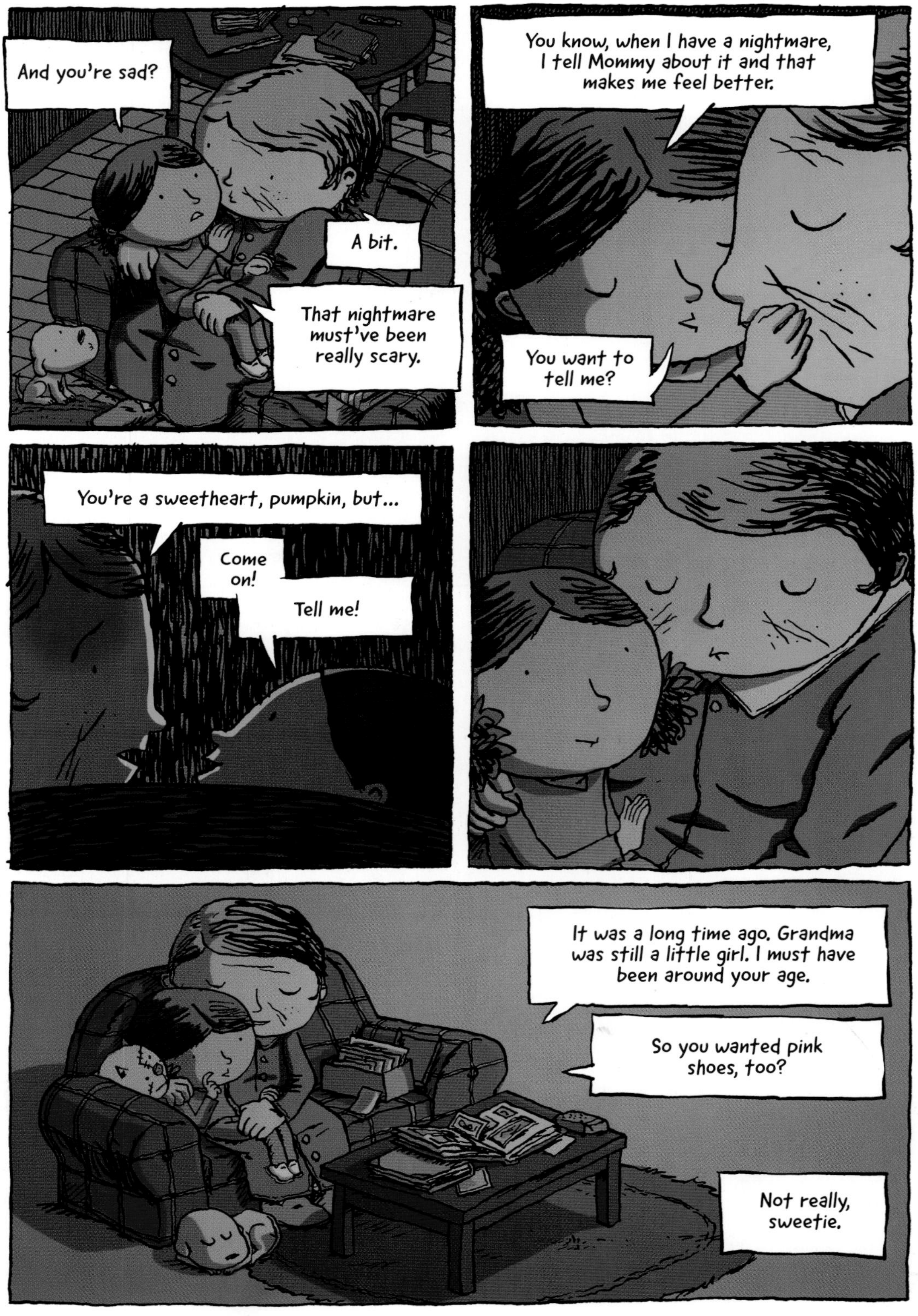
And you're sad?
A bit.
That nightmare must've been really scary.
You know, when I have a nightmare, I tell Mommy about it and that makes me feel better.
You want to tell me?
You're a sweetheart, pumpkin, but...
Come on!
Tell me!
It was a long time ago. Grandma was still a little girl. I must have been around your age.
So you wanted pink shoes, too?
Not really, sweetie.

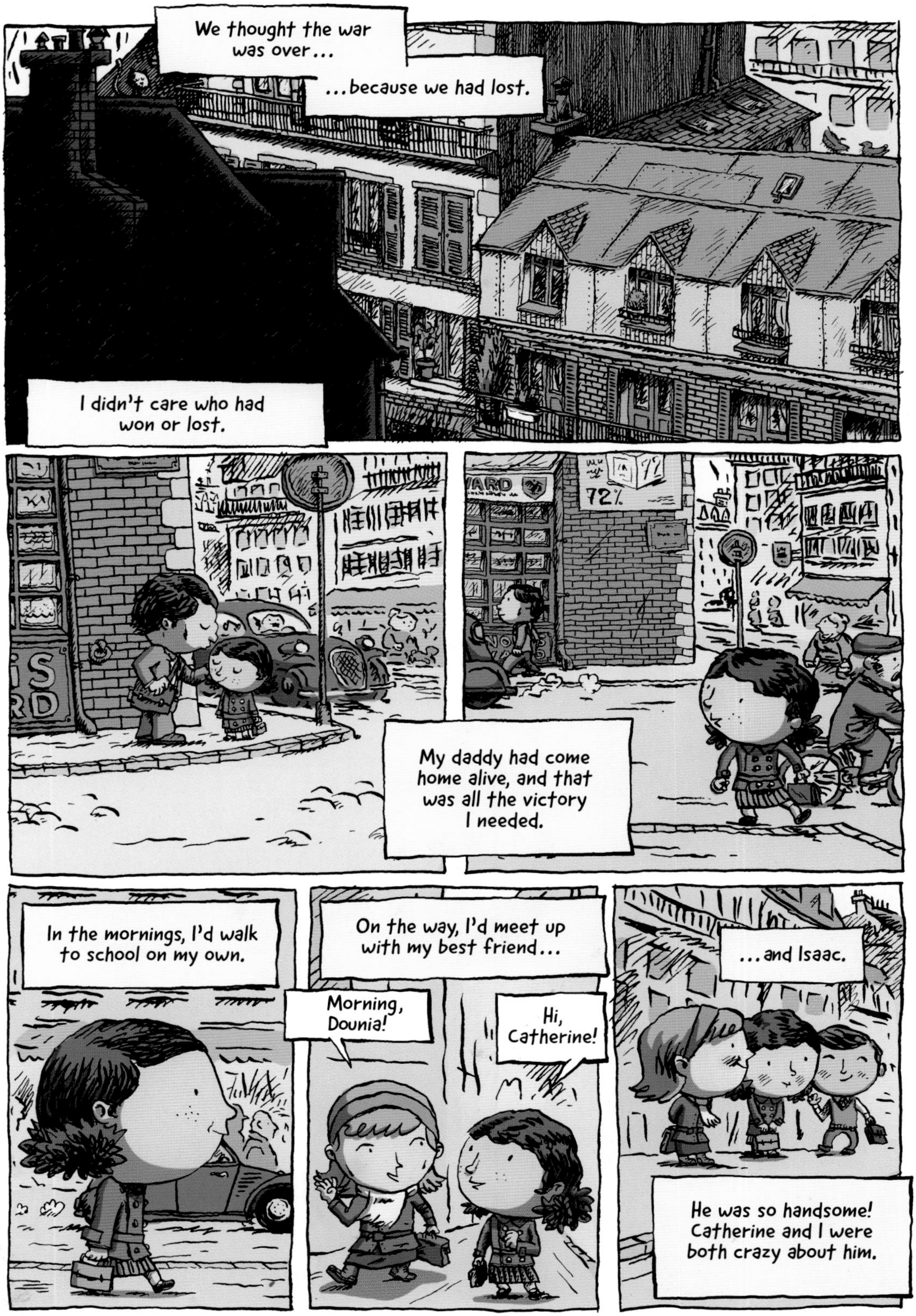
We thought the war was over...
...because we had lost.
I didn't care who had won or lost.
My daddy had come home alive, and that was all the victory I needed.
In the mornings, I'd walk to school on my own.
On the way, I'd meet up with my best friend...
Morning, Dounia!
Hi, Catherine!
...and Isaac.
He was so handsome! Catherine and I were both crazy about him.

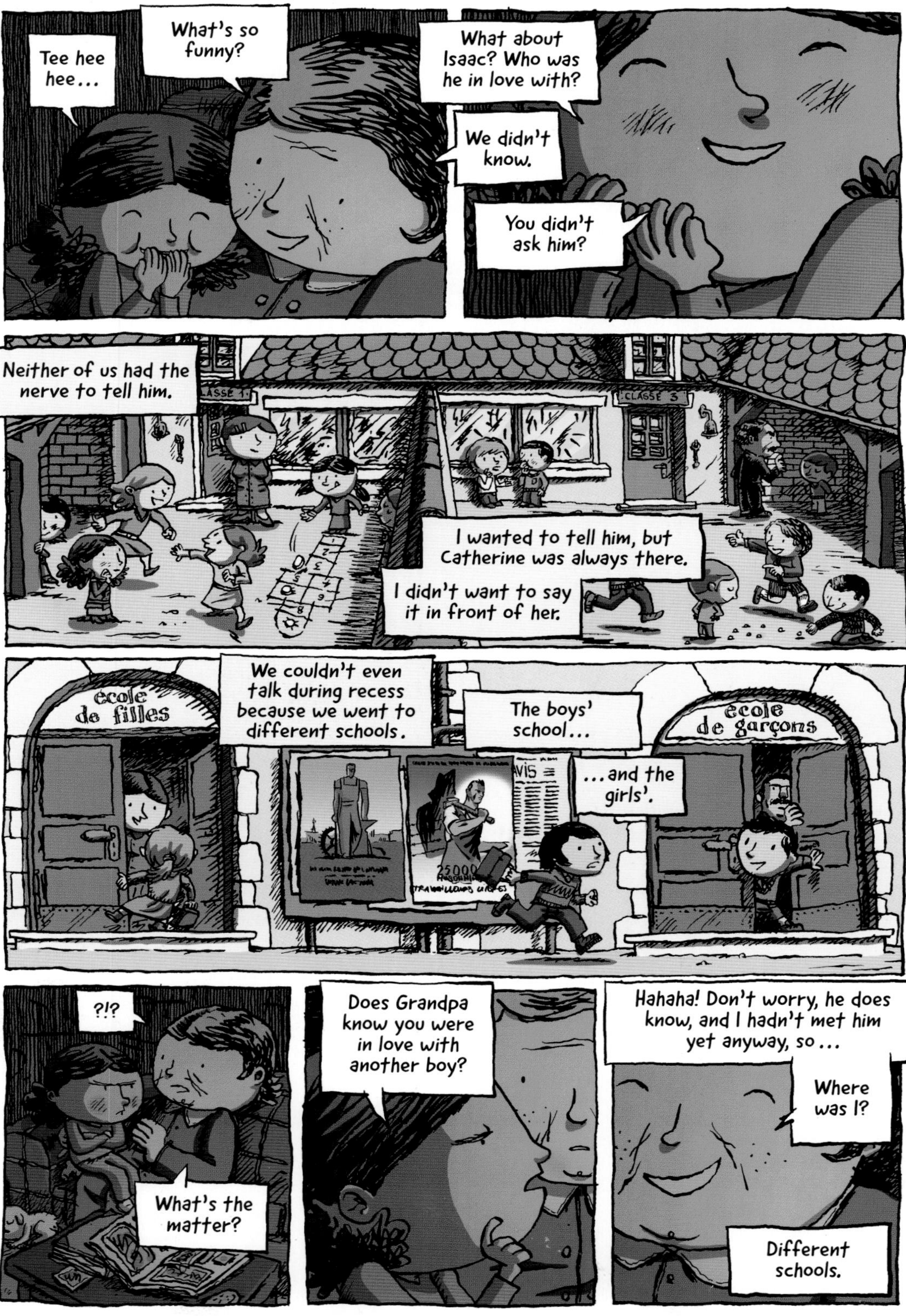
Tee hee hee...
What's so funny?
What about Isaac? Who was he in love with?
We didn't know.
You didn't ask him?
Neither of us had the nerve to tell him.
CLASSE 1
CLASSE 3
I wanted to tell him, but Catherine was always there.
I didn't want to say it in front of her.
école de filles
We couldn't even talk during recess because we went to different schools.
The boys' school...
AVIS
...and the girls'.
école de garçons
?!?
What's the matter?
Does Grandpa know you were in love with another boy?
Hahaha! Don't worry, he does know, and I hadn't met him yet anyway, so...
Where was I?
Different schools.

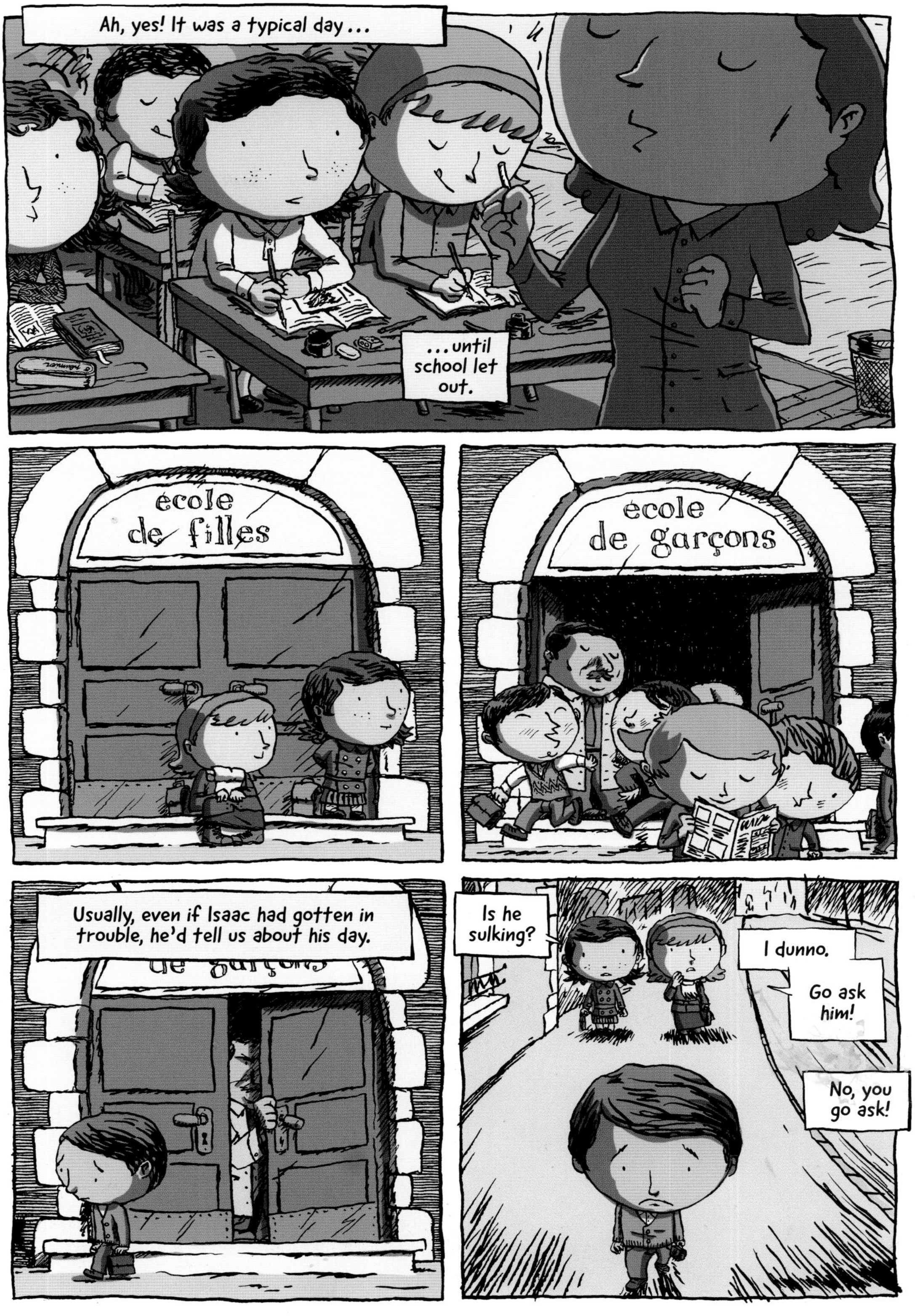
Ah, yes! It was a typical day . . .
. . . until school let out.
école de filles
école de garçons
Usually, even if Isaac had gotten in trouble, he'd tell us about his day.
Is he sulking?
I dunno.
Go ask him!
No, you go ask!

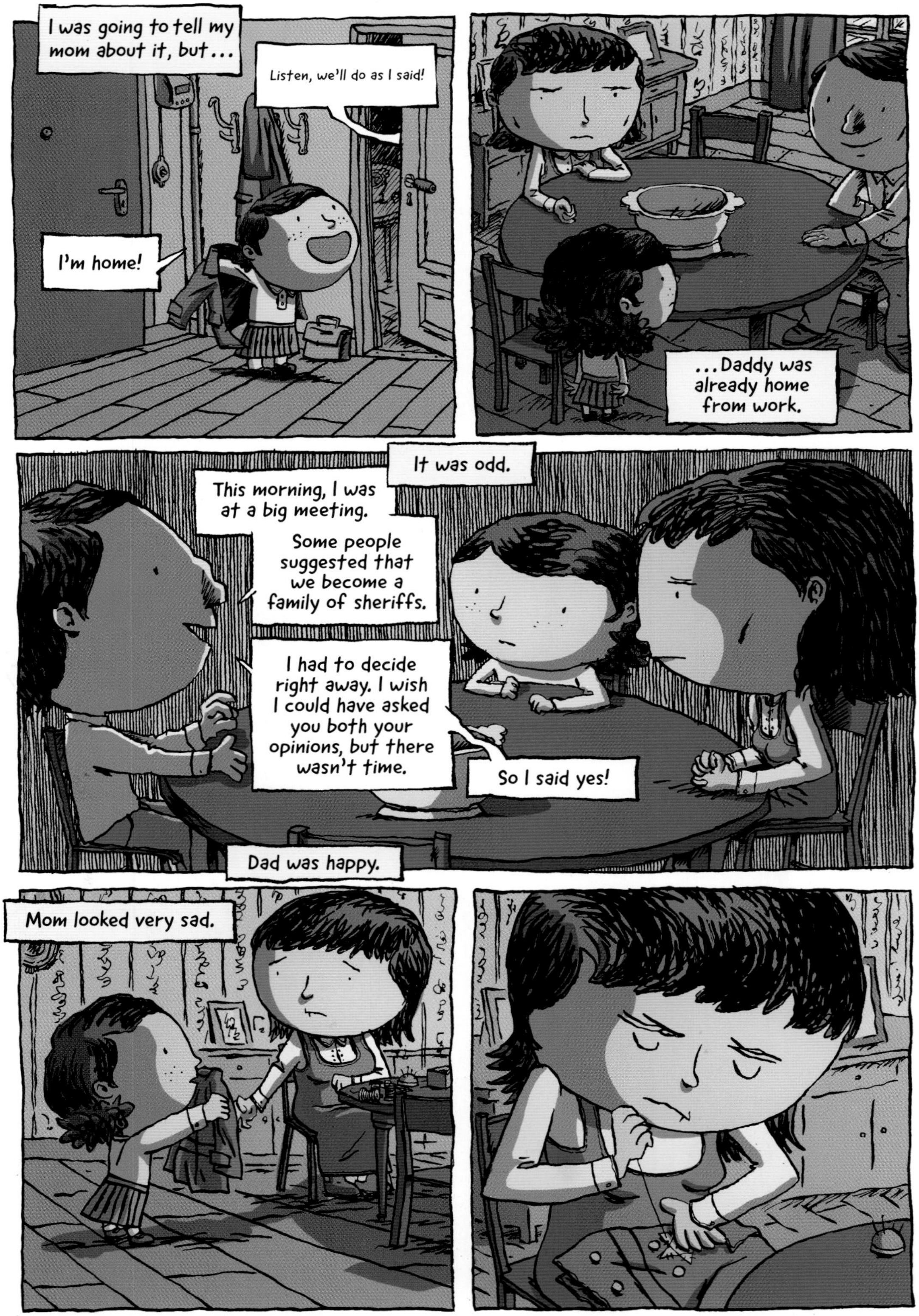
I was going to tell my mom about it, but...
Listen, we'll do as I said!
I'm home!
...Daddy was already home from work.
It was odd.
This morning, I was at a big meeting.
Some people suggested that we become a family of sheriffs.
I had to decide right away. I wish I could have asked you both your opinions, but there wasn't time.
So I said yes!
Dad was happy.
Mom looked very sad.

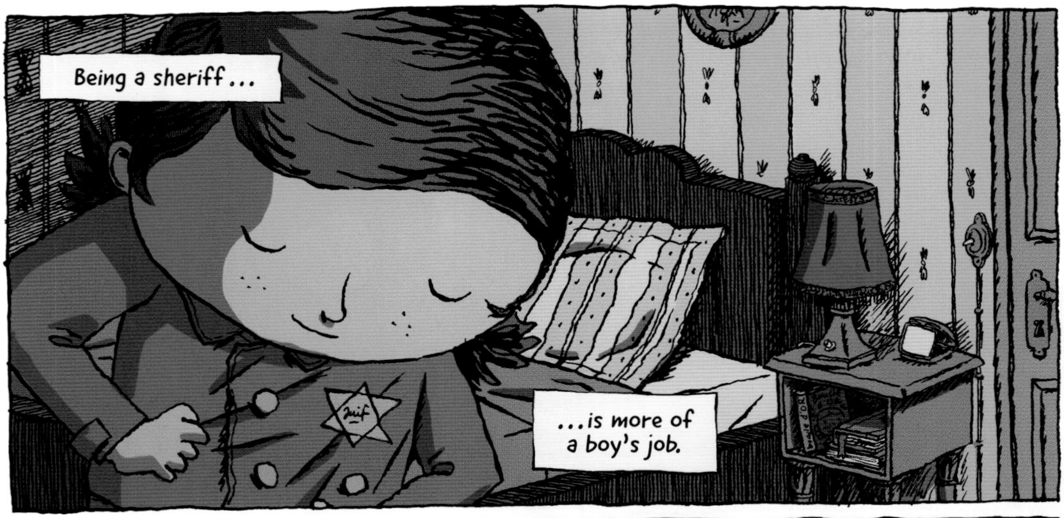
Being a sheriff...
Juif
...is more of a boy's job.

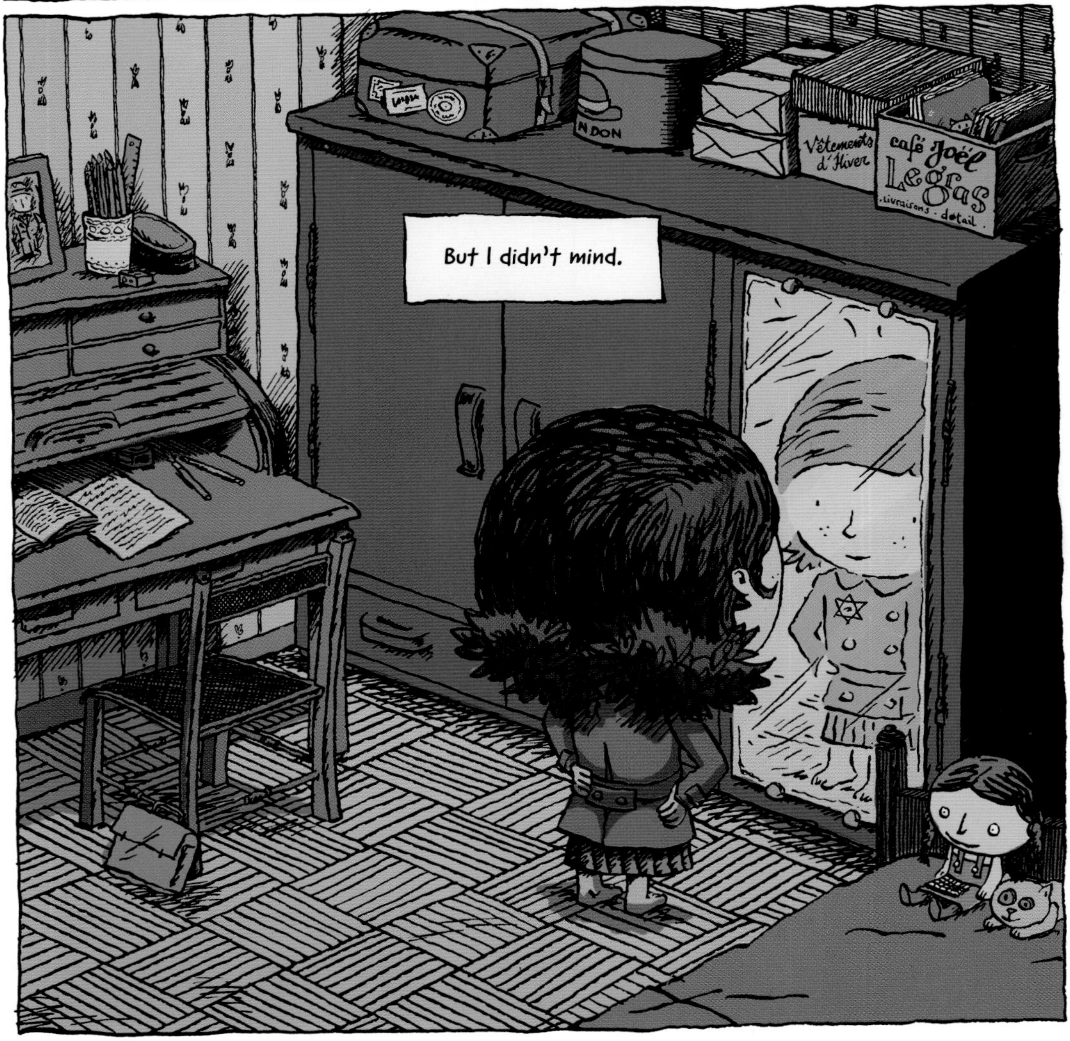
N DON
Vêtements d'Hiver
café Joël Legras
livraisons · détail
But I didn't mind.

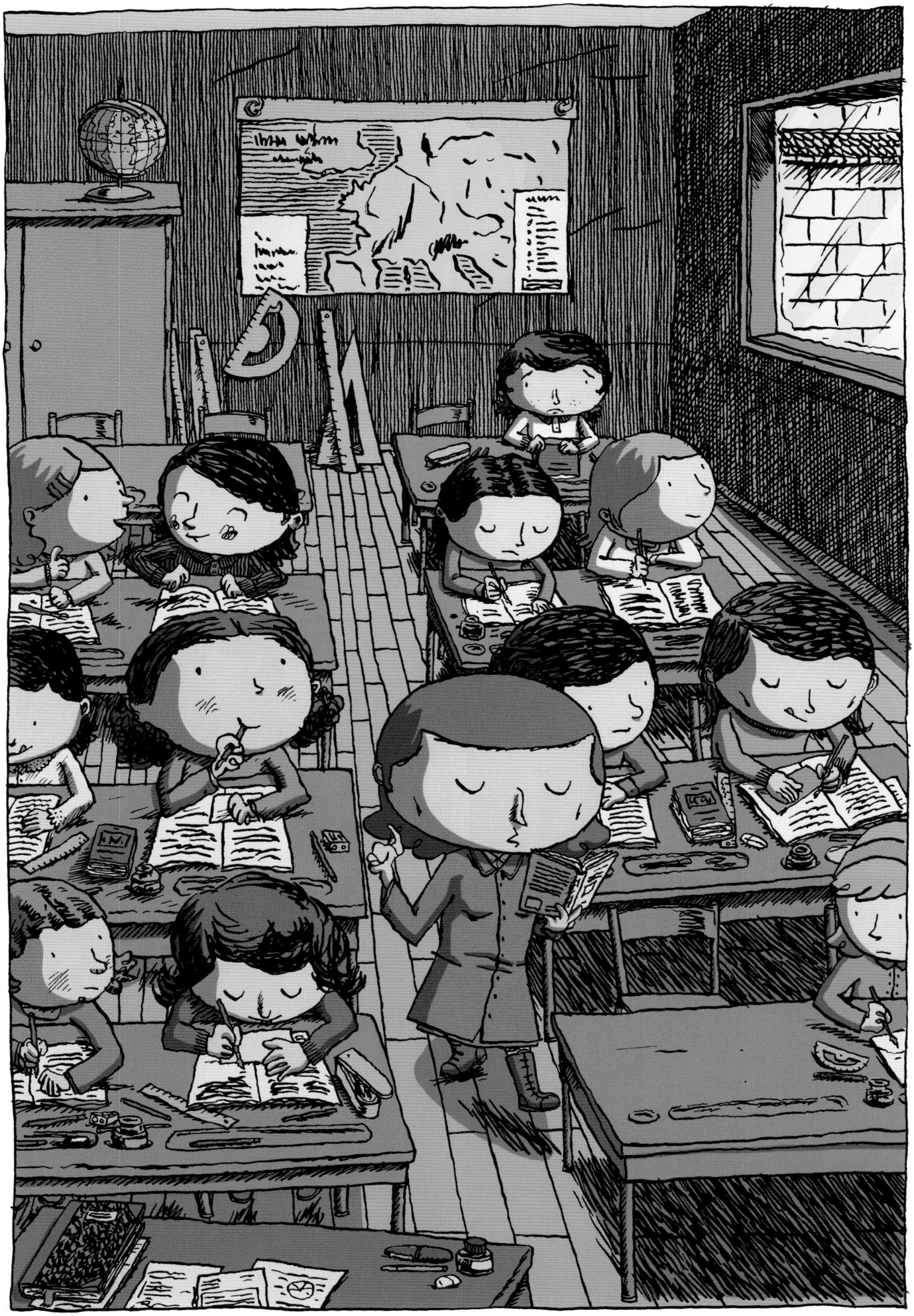

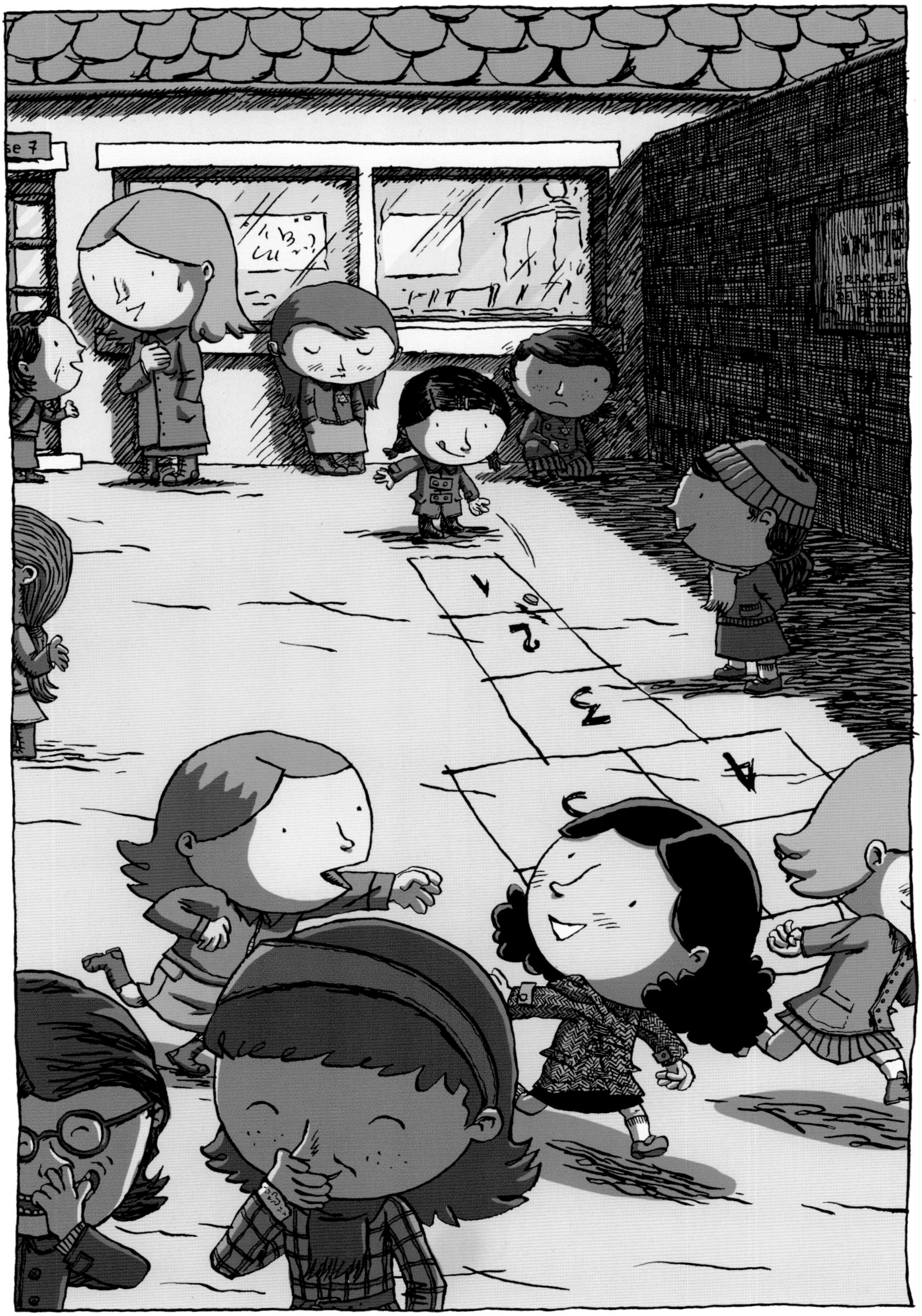
se 7

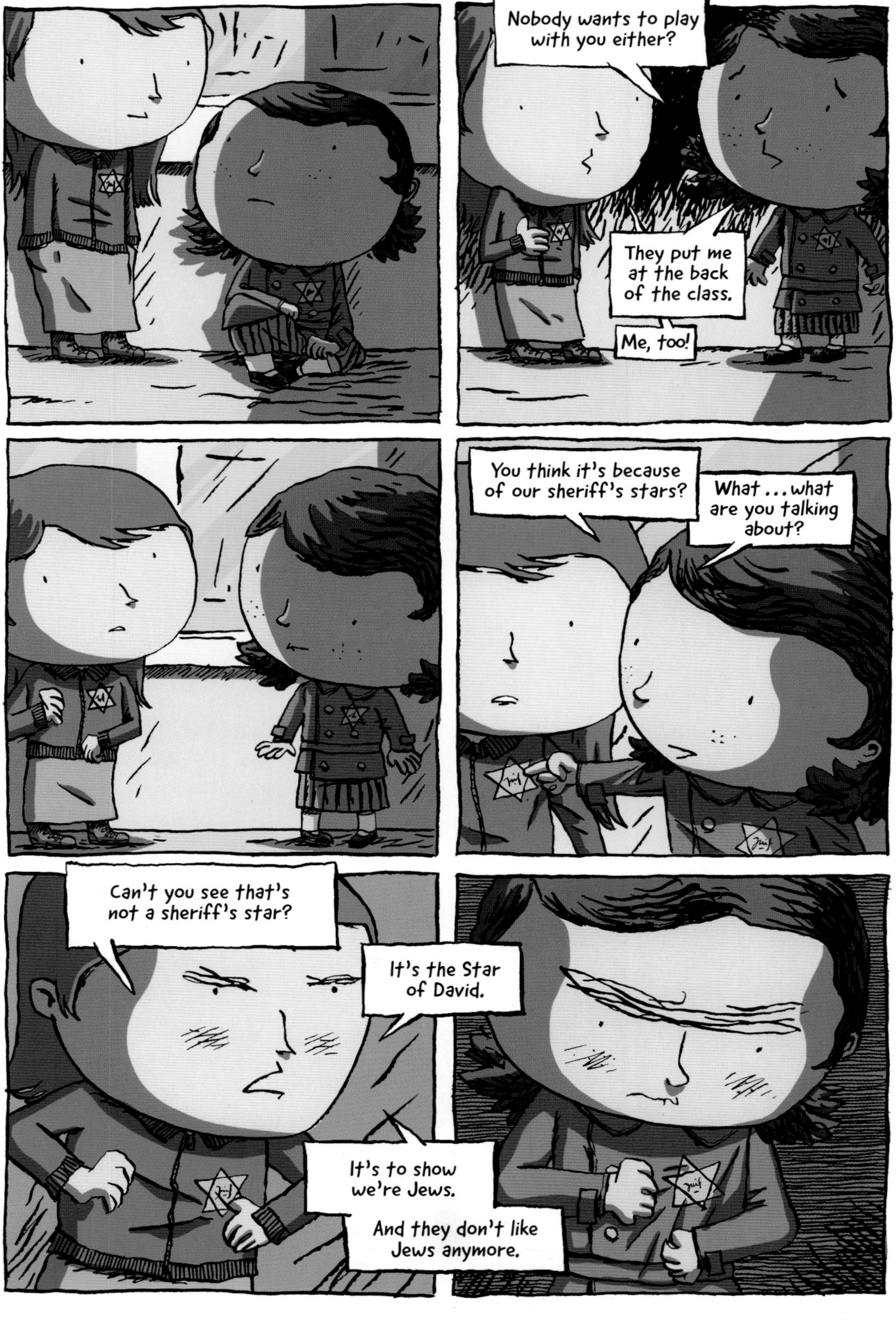
Nobody wants to play with you either?
They put me at the back of the class.
Me, too!
You think it's because of our sheriff's stars?
What ... what are you talking about?
Can't you see that's not a sheriff's star?
It's the Star of David.
It's to show we're Jews.
And they don't like Jews anymore.

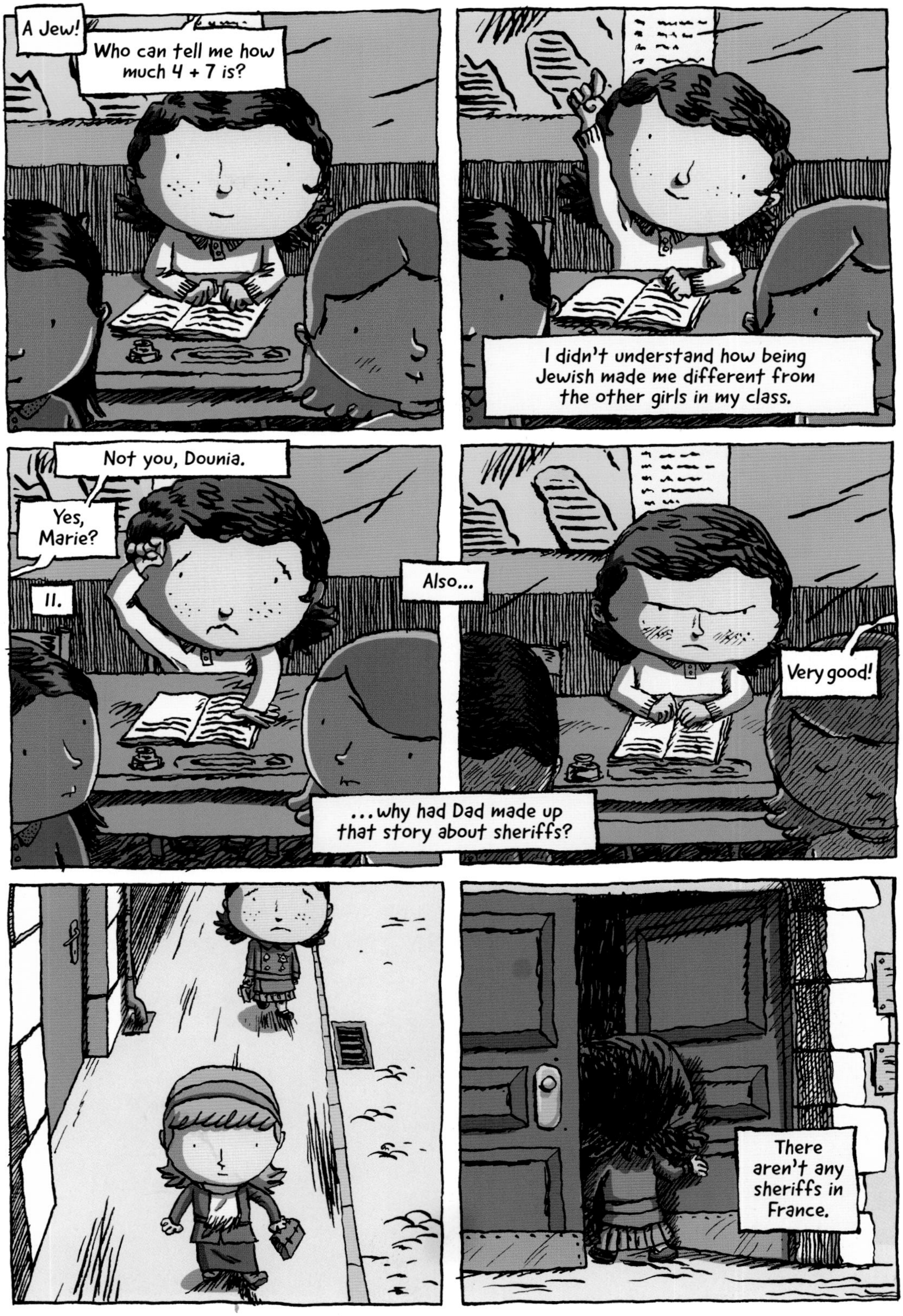
A Jew!
Who can tell me how much 4 + 7 is?
I didn't understand how being Jewish made me different from the other girls in my class.
Not you, Dounia.
Yes, Marie?
11.
Also...
Very good!
...why had Dad made up that story about sheriffs?
There aren't any sheriffs in France.

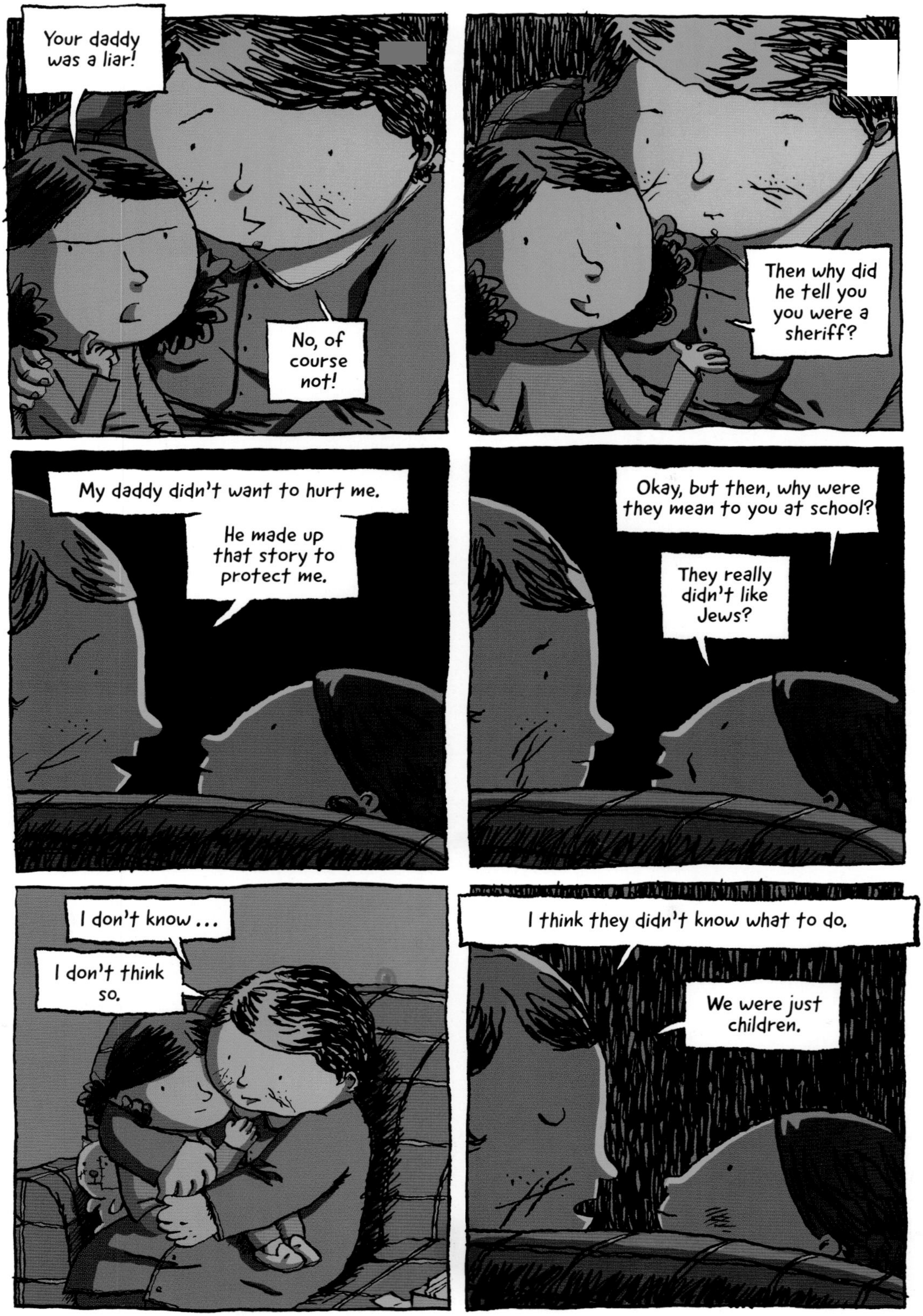
Your daddy was a liar!
No, of course not!
Then why did he tell you you were a sheriff?
My daddy didn't want to hurt me.
He made up that story to protect me.
Okay, but then, why were they mean to you at school?
They really didn't like Jews?
I don't know...
I don't think so.
I think they didn't know what to do.
We were just children.

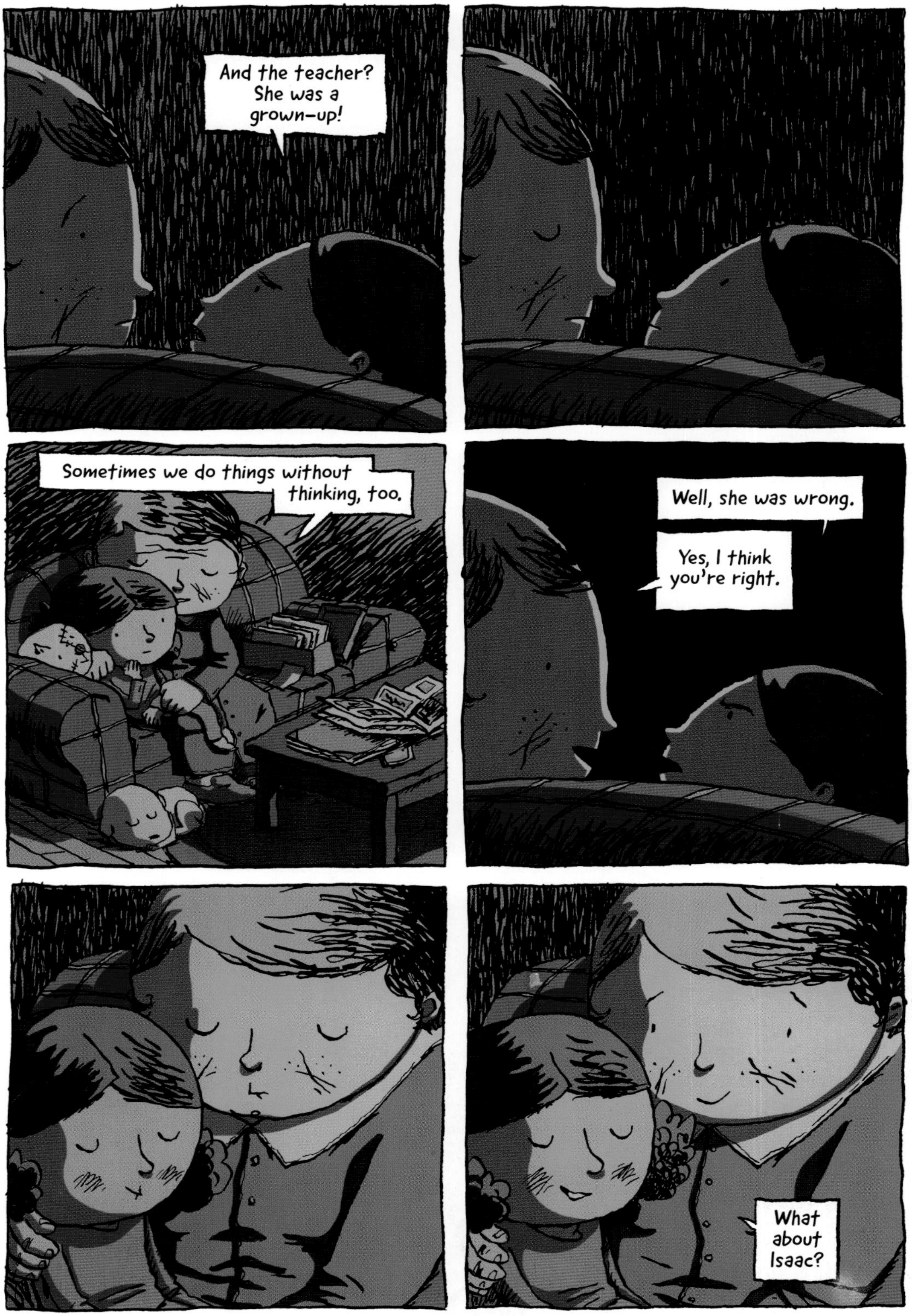
And the teacher? She was a grown-up!
Sometimes we do things without thinking, too.
Well, she was wrong.
Yes, I think you're right.
What about Isaac?

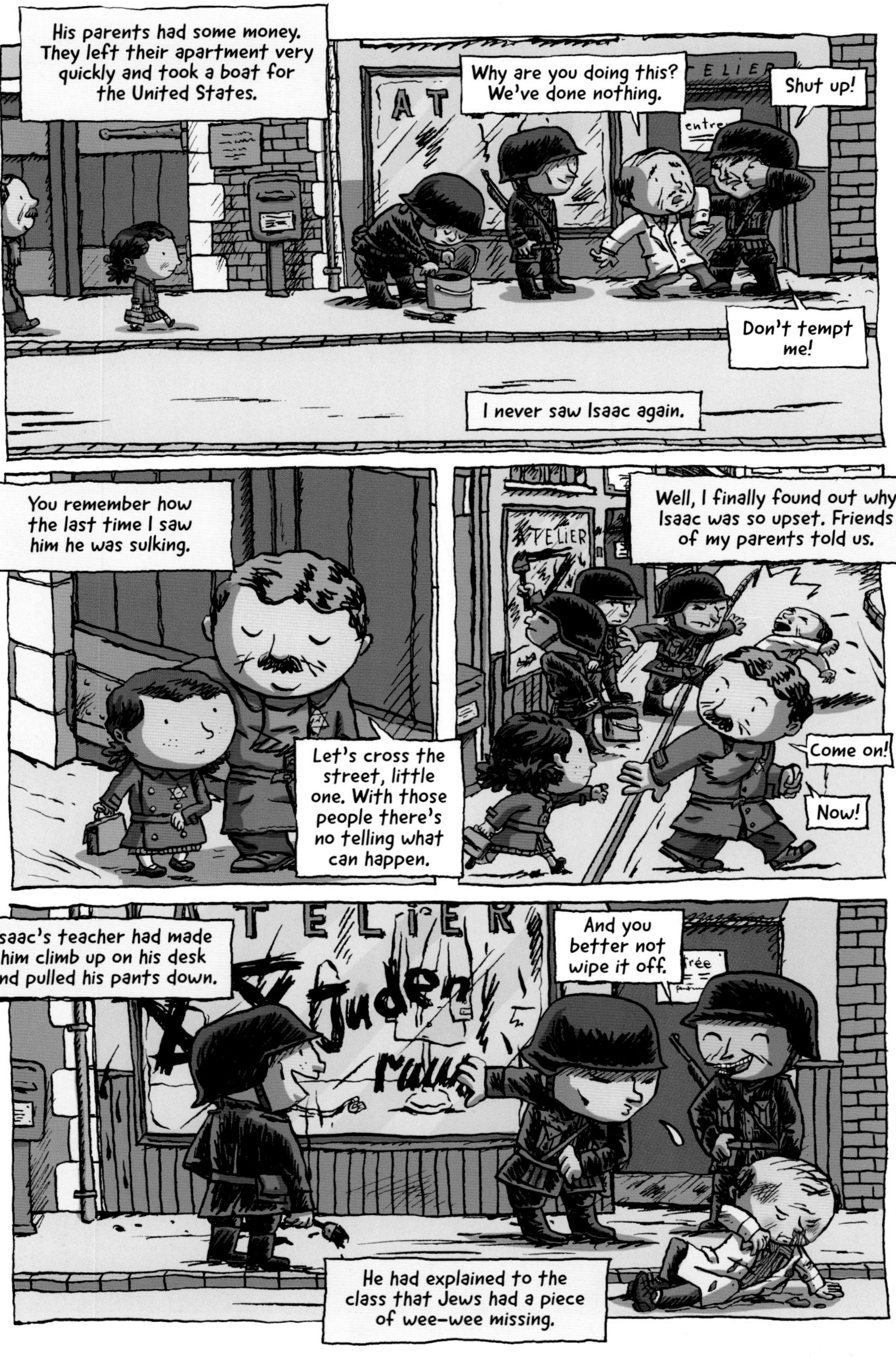
His parents had some money. They left their apartment very quickly and took a boat for the United States.
Why are you doing this? We've done nothing.
Shut up!
Don't tempt me!
I never saw Isaac again.
You remember how the last time I saw him he was sulking.
Let's cross the street, little one. With those people there's no telling what can happen.
Well, I finally found out why Isaac was so upset. Friends of my parents told us.
Come on!
Now!
Isaac's teacher had made him climb up on his desk and pulled his pants down.
And you better not wipe it off.
He had explained to the class that Jews had a piece of wee-wee missing.

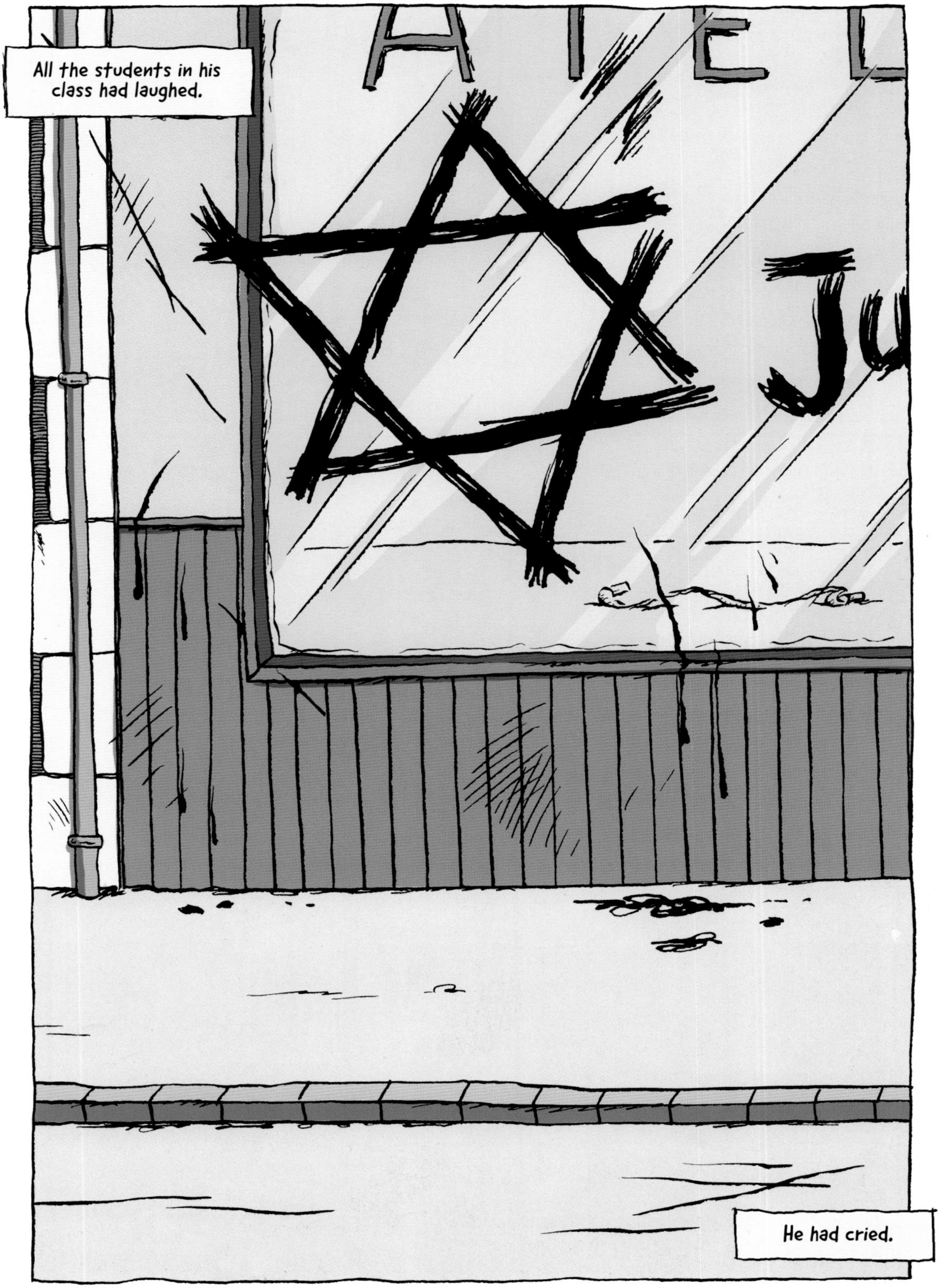
All the students in his class had laughed.
He had cried.

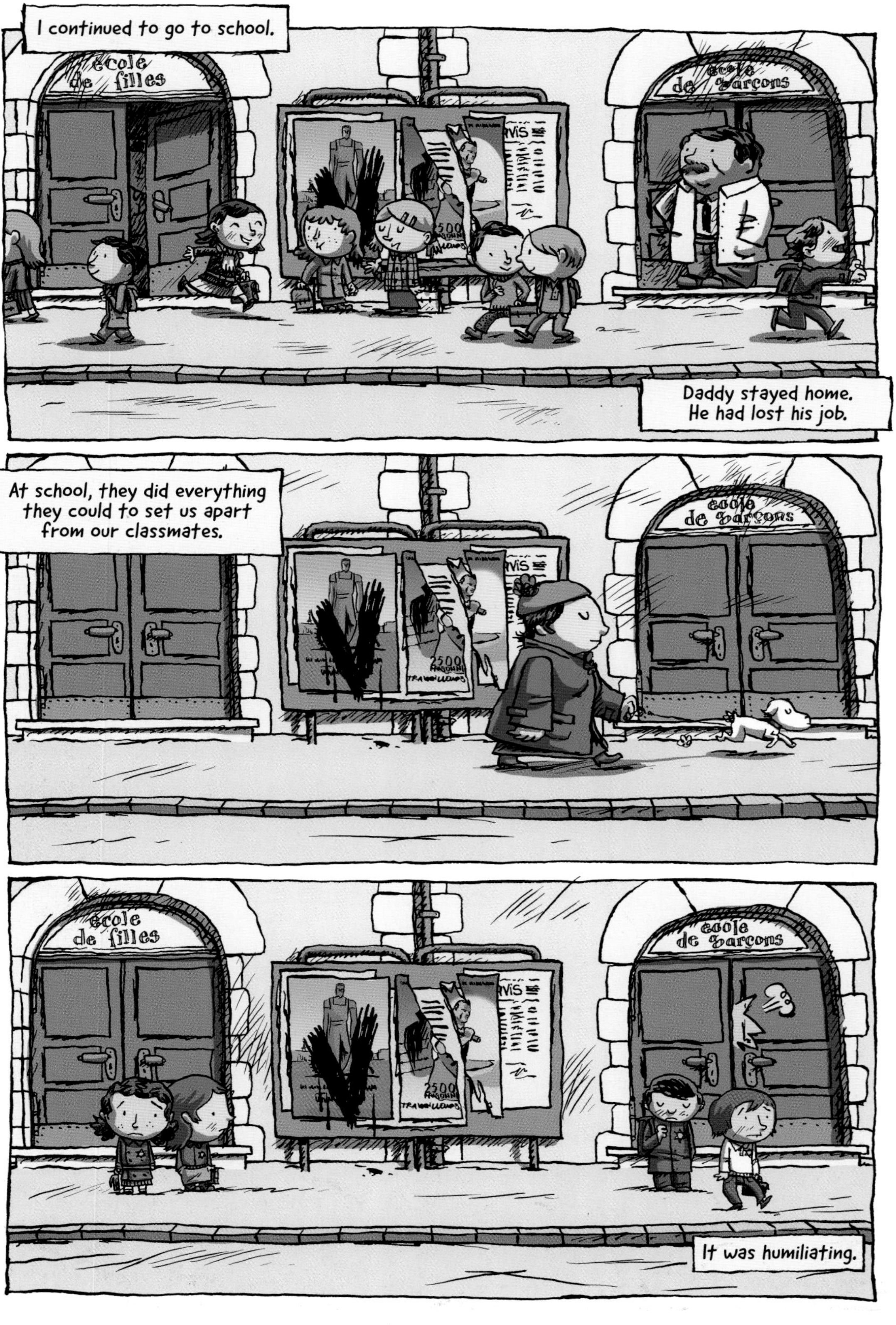
I continued to go to school.
école de filles
école de garçons
AVIS
Daddy stayed home. He had lost his job.
At school, they did everything they could to set us apart from our classmates.
école de garçons
école de filles
école de garçons
It was humiliating.

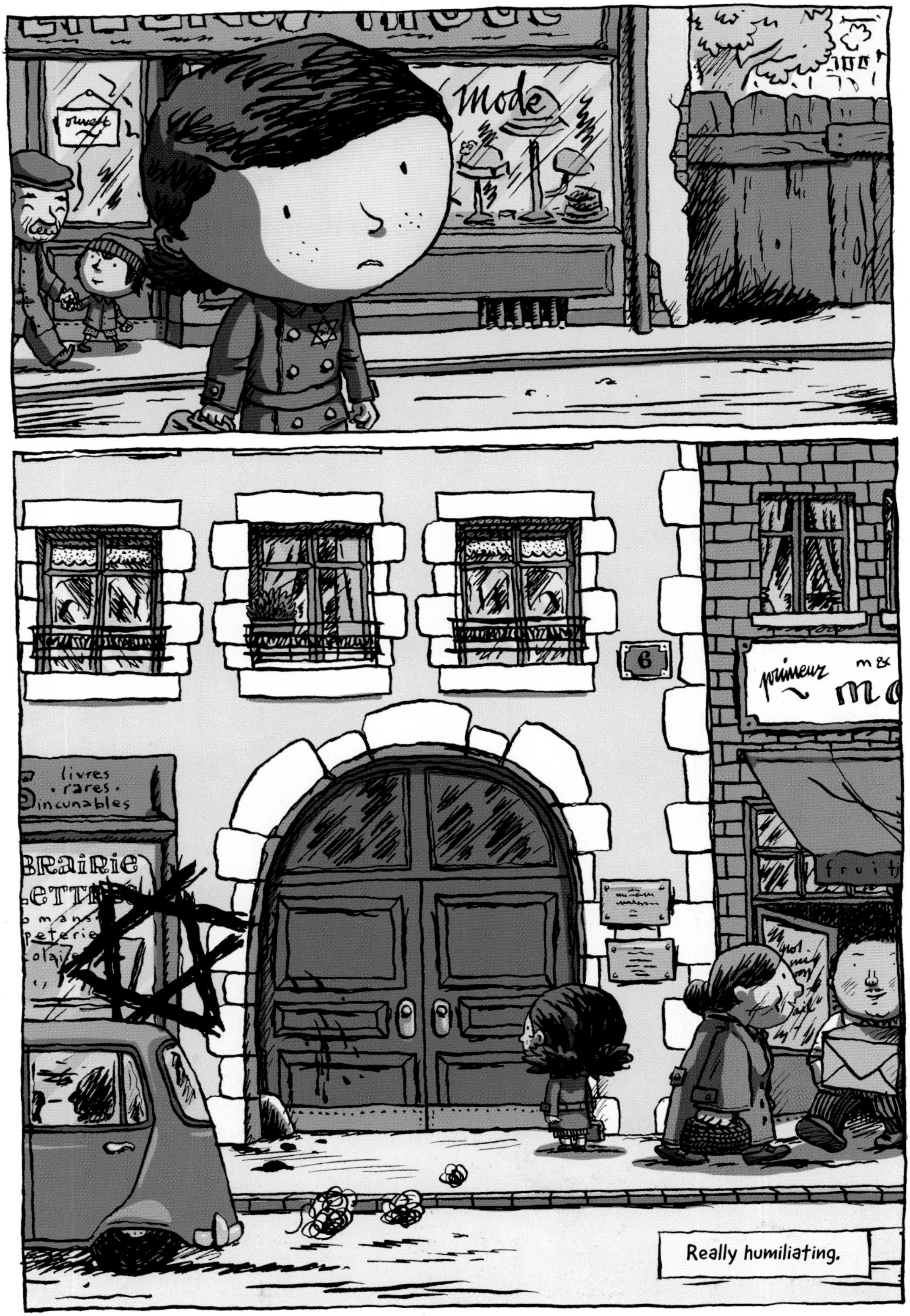
ouvert
mode
6
livres
rares
incunables
Really humiliating.

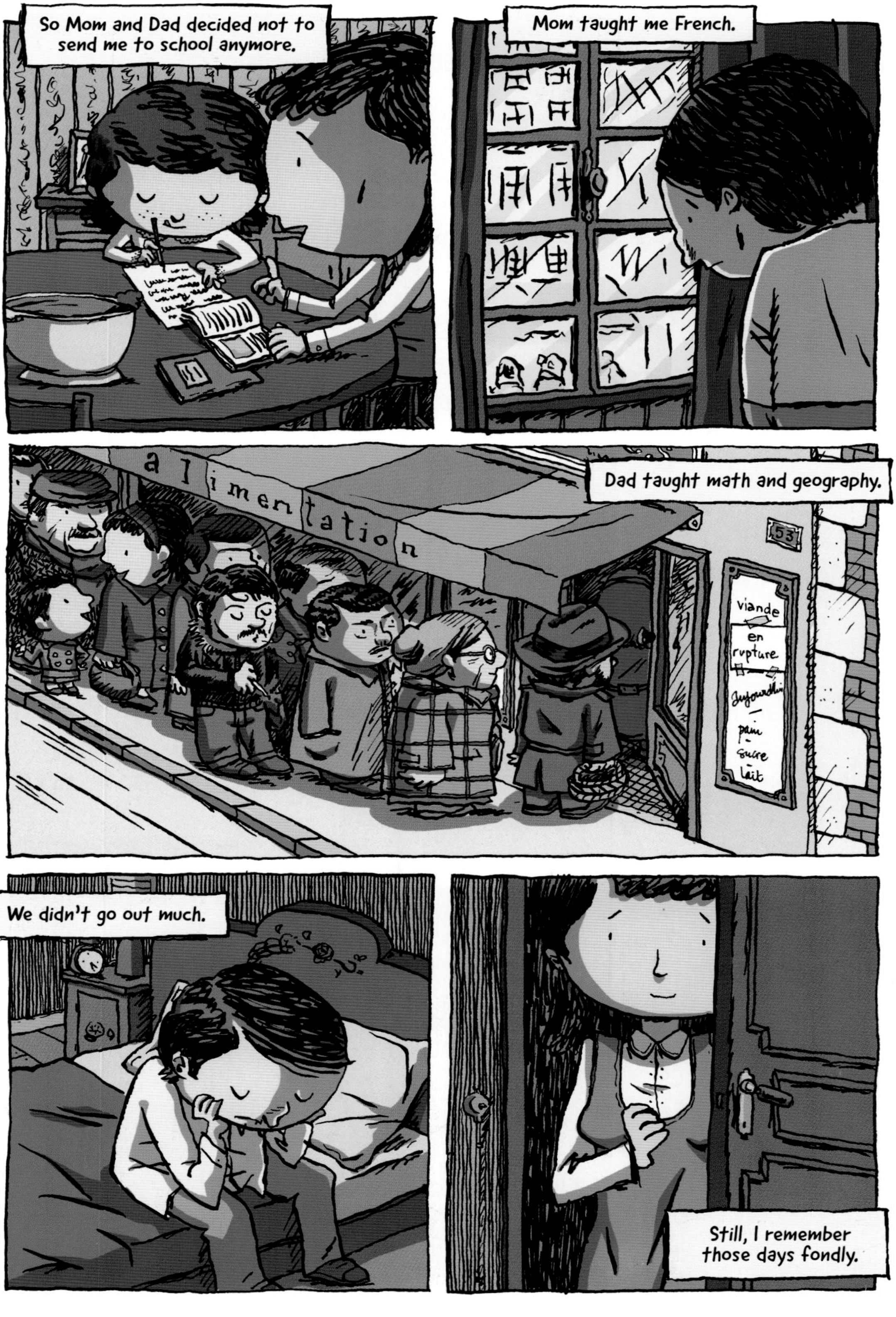
So Mom and Dad decided not to send me to school anymore.
Mom taught me French.
alimentation
Dad taught math and geography.
53
viande
en rupture
pain
sucre
lait
We didn't go out much.
Still, I remember those days fondly.

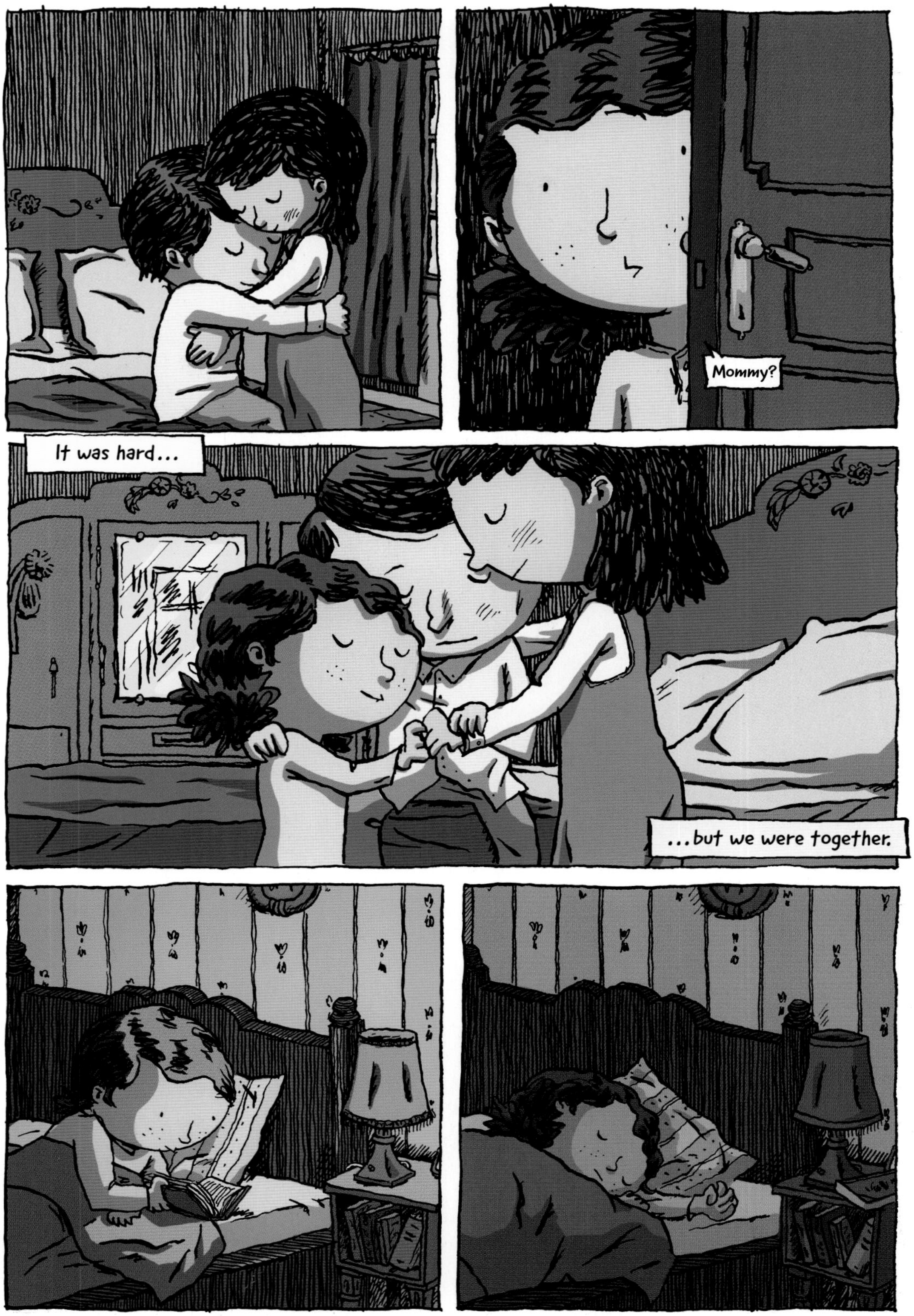
Mommy?
It was hard...
...but we were together.

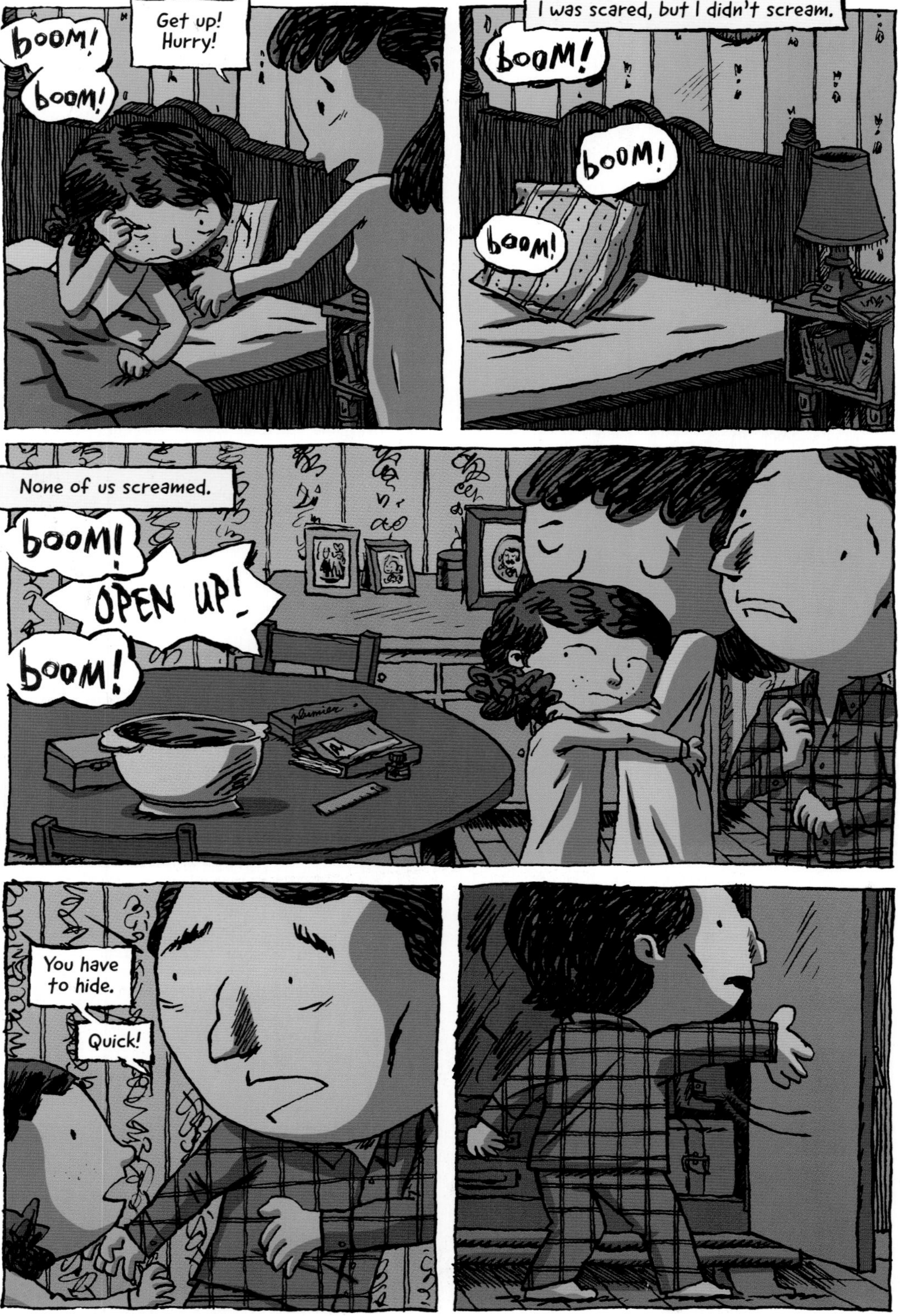
boom!
boom!
Get up! Hurry!
I was scared, but I didn't scream.
boom!
boom!
boom!
None of us screamed.
boom!
OPEN UP!
boom!
plumier
You have to hide.
Quick!

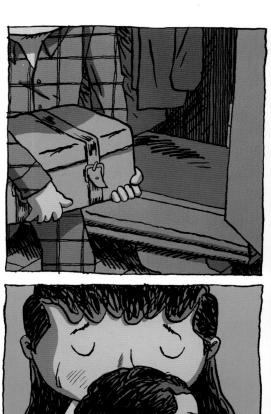

Listen to me, sweetheart. Mommy loves you very much. I will always love you.

Dounia! Hurry!

25

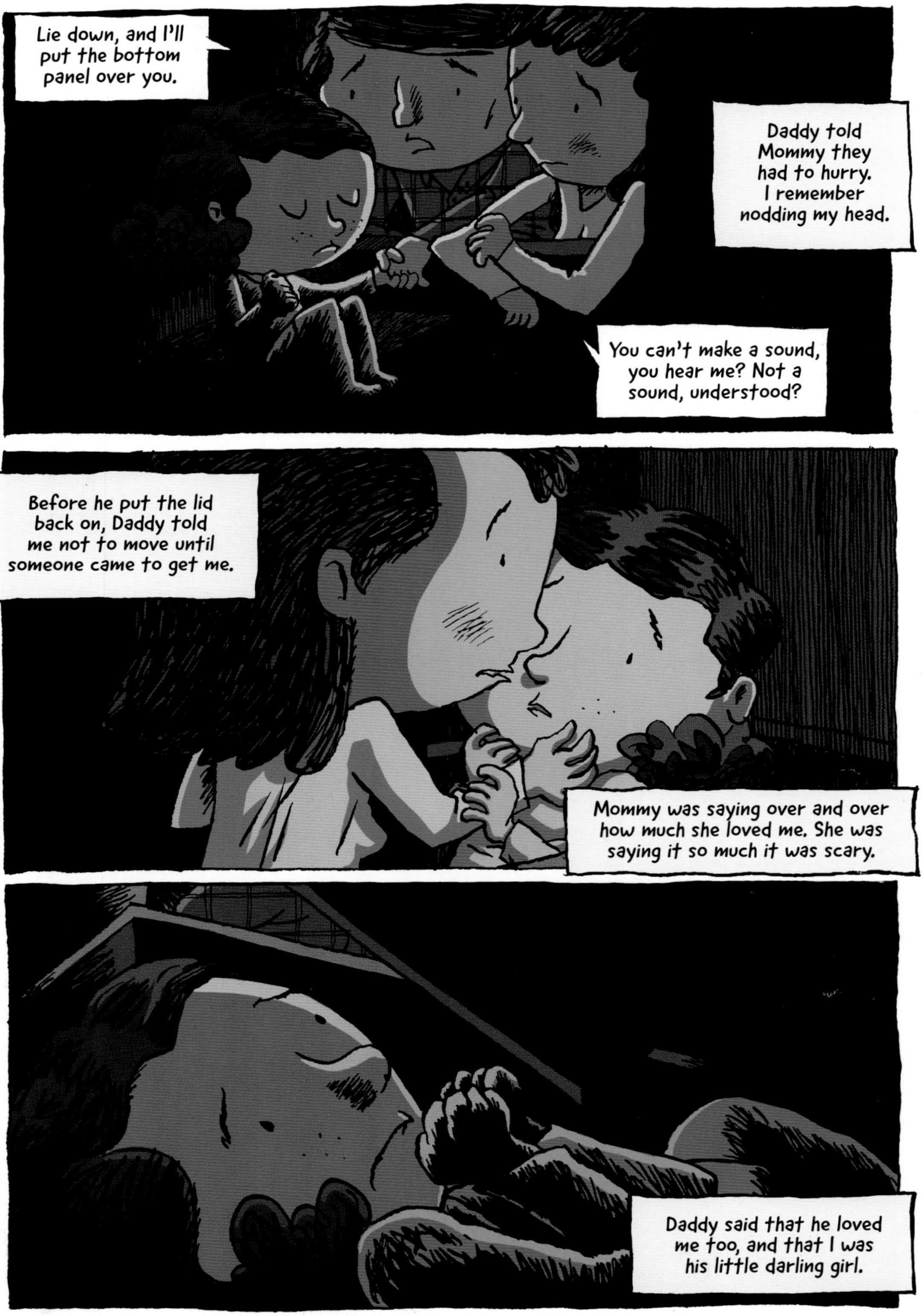
Lie down, and I'll put the bottom panel over you.
Daddy told Mommy they had to hurry. I remember nodding my head.
You can't make a sound, you hear me? Not a sound, understood?
Before he put the lid back on, Daddy told me not to move until someone came to get me.
Mommy was saying over and over how much she loved me. She was saying it so much it was scary.
Daddy said that he loved me too, and that I was his little darling girl.

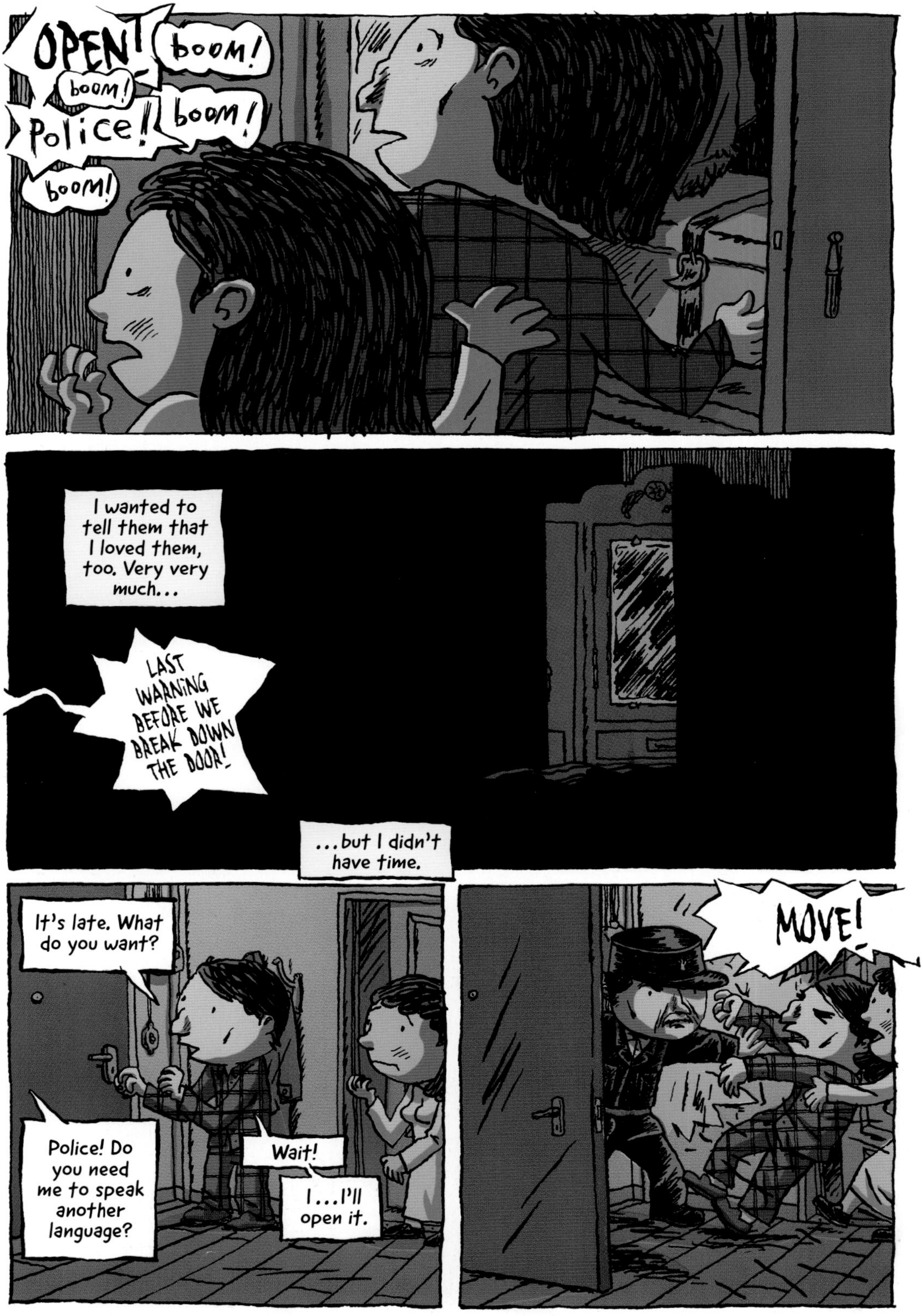
OPEN!
boom!
boom!
Police!
boom!
boom!
I wanted to tell them that I loved them, too. Very very much...
LAST WARNING BEFORE WE BREAK DOWN THE DOOR!
...but I didn't have time.
It's late. What do you want?
Police! Do you need me to speak another language?
Wait!
I...I'll open it.
MOVE!

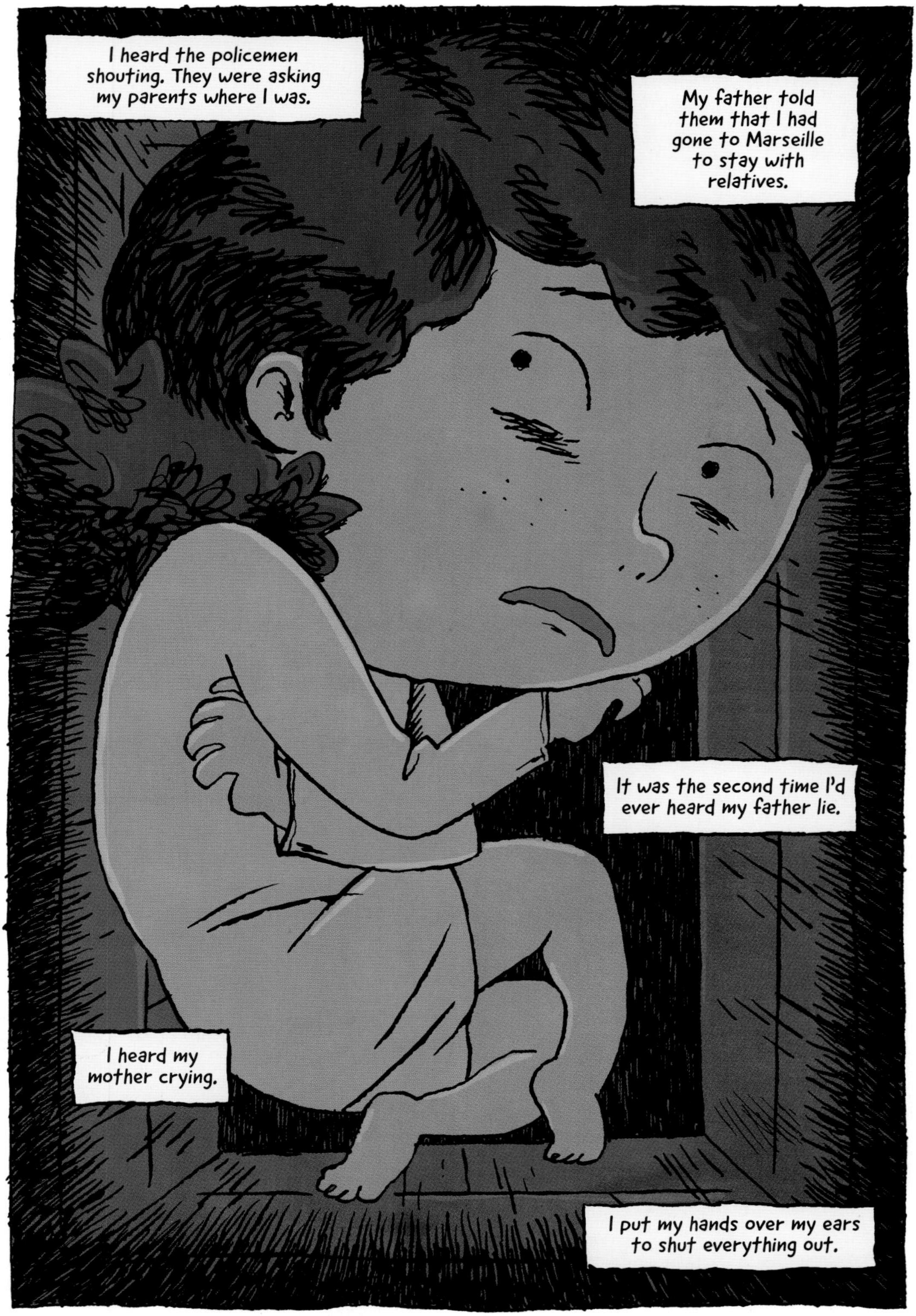
I heard the policemen shouting. They were asking my parents where I was.
My father told them that I had gone to Marseille to stay with relatives.
It was the second time I'd ever heard my father lie.
I heard my mother crying.
I put my hands over my ears to shut everything out.

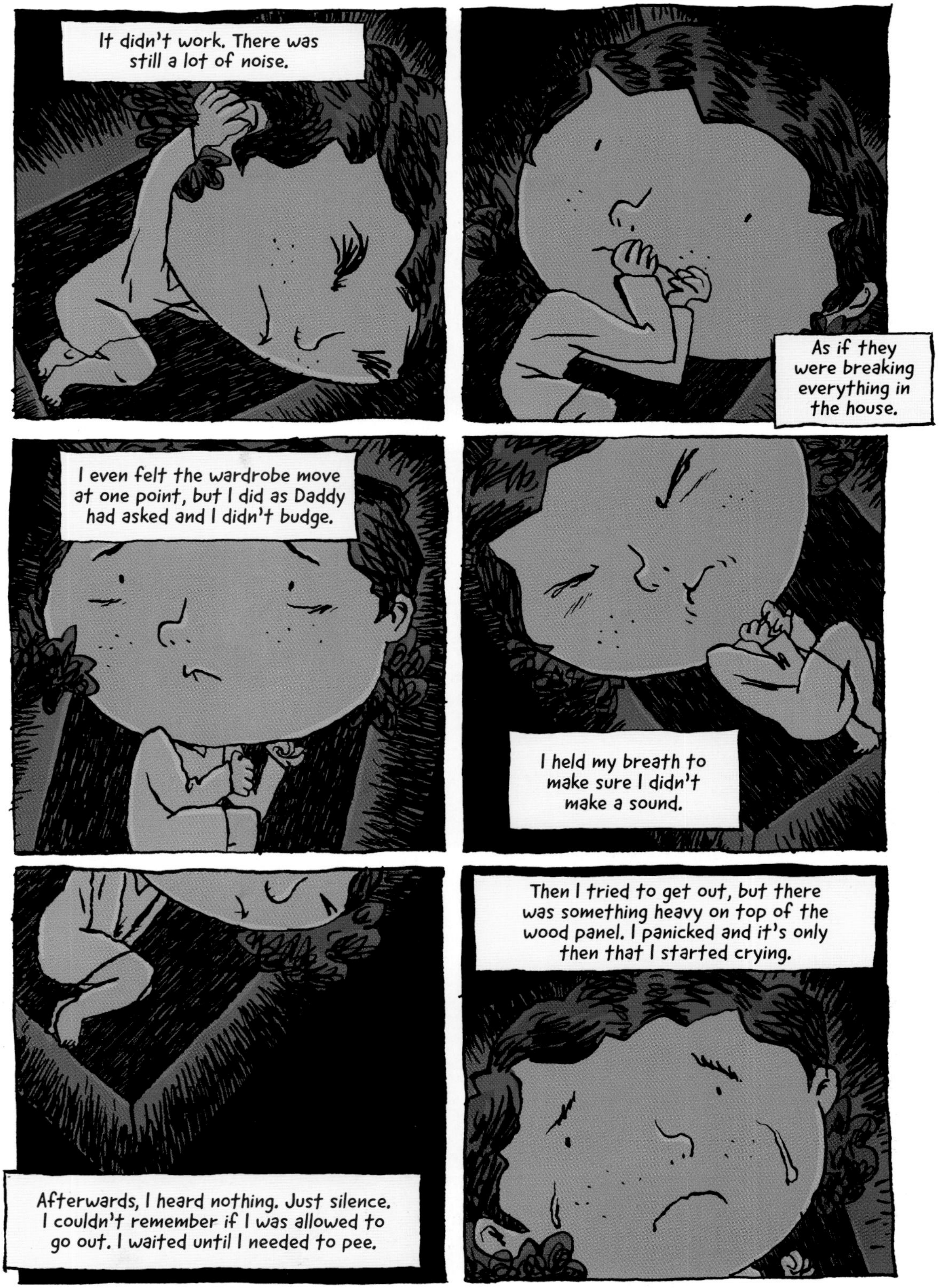
It didn't work. There was still a lot of noise.
As if they were breaking everything in the house.
I even felt the wardrobe move at one point, but I did as Daddy had asked and I didn't budge.
I held my breath to make sure I didn't make a sound.
Afterwards, I heard nothing. Just silence. I couldn't remember if I was allowed to go out. I waited until I needed to pee.
Then I tried to get out, but there was something heavy on top of the wood panel. I panicked and it's only then that I started crying.

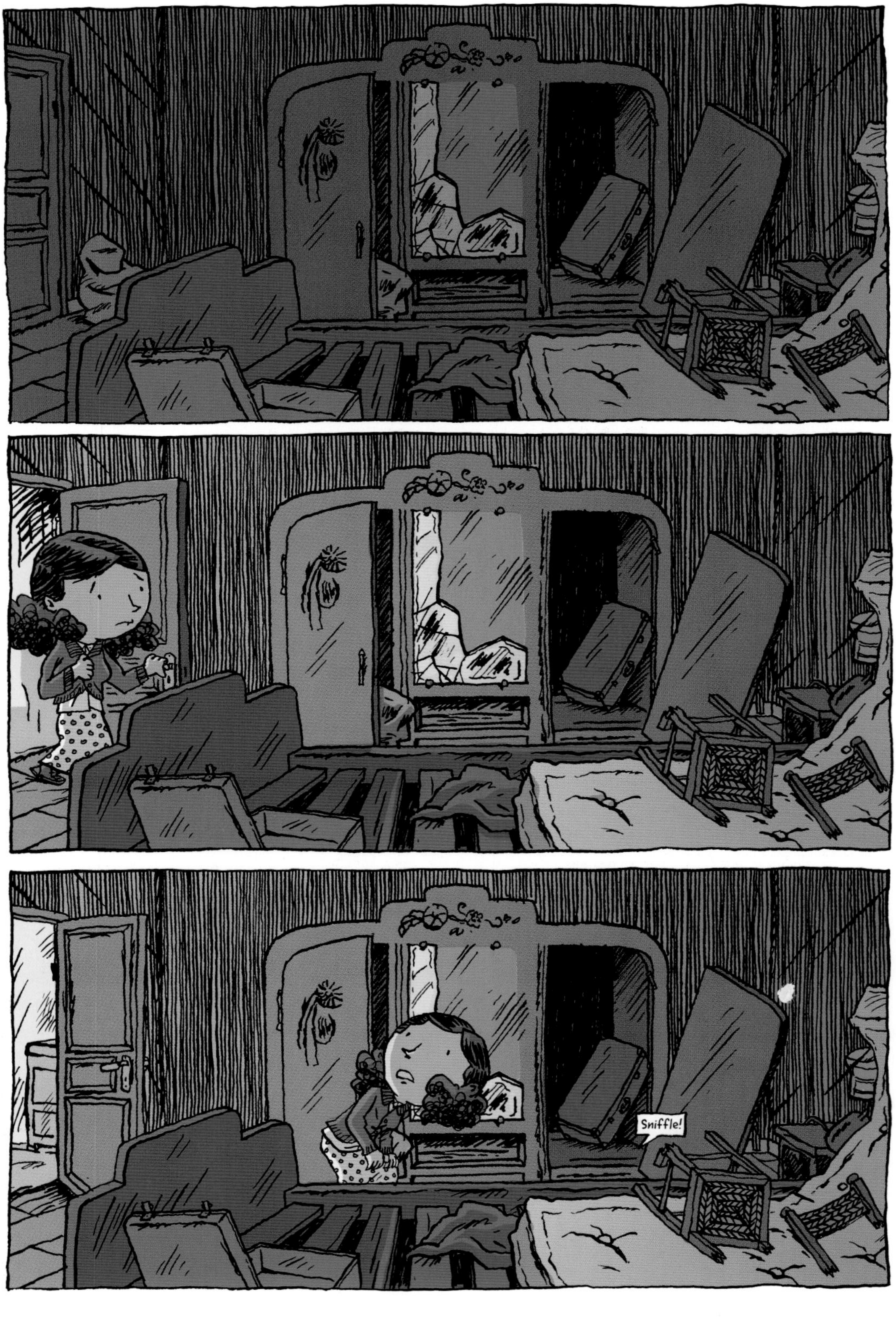
Sniffle!

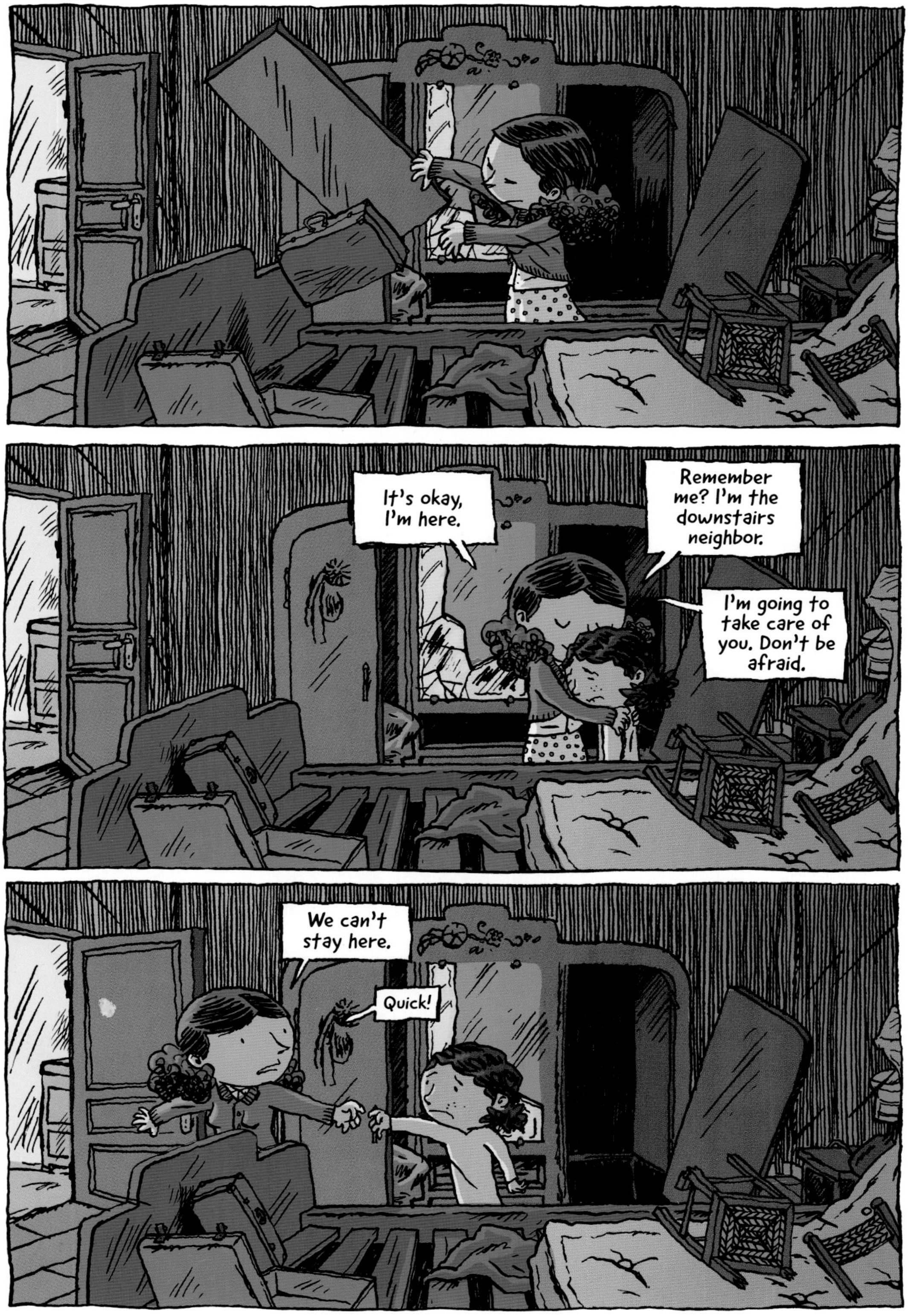
It's okay, I'm here.
Remember me? I'm the downstairs neighbor.
I'm going to take care of you. Don't be afraid.
We can't stay here.
Quick!

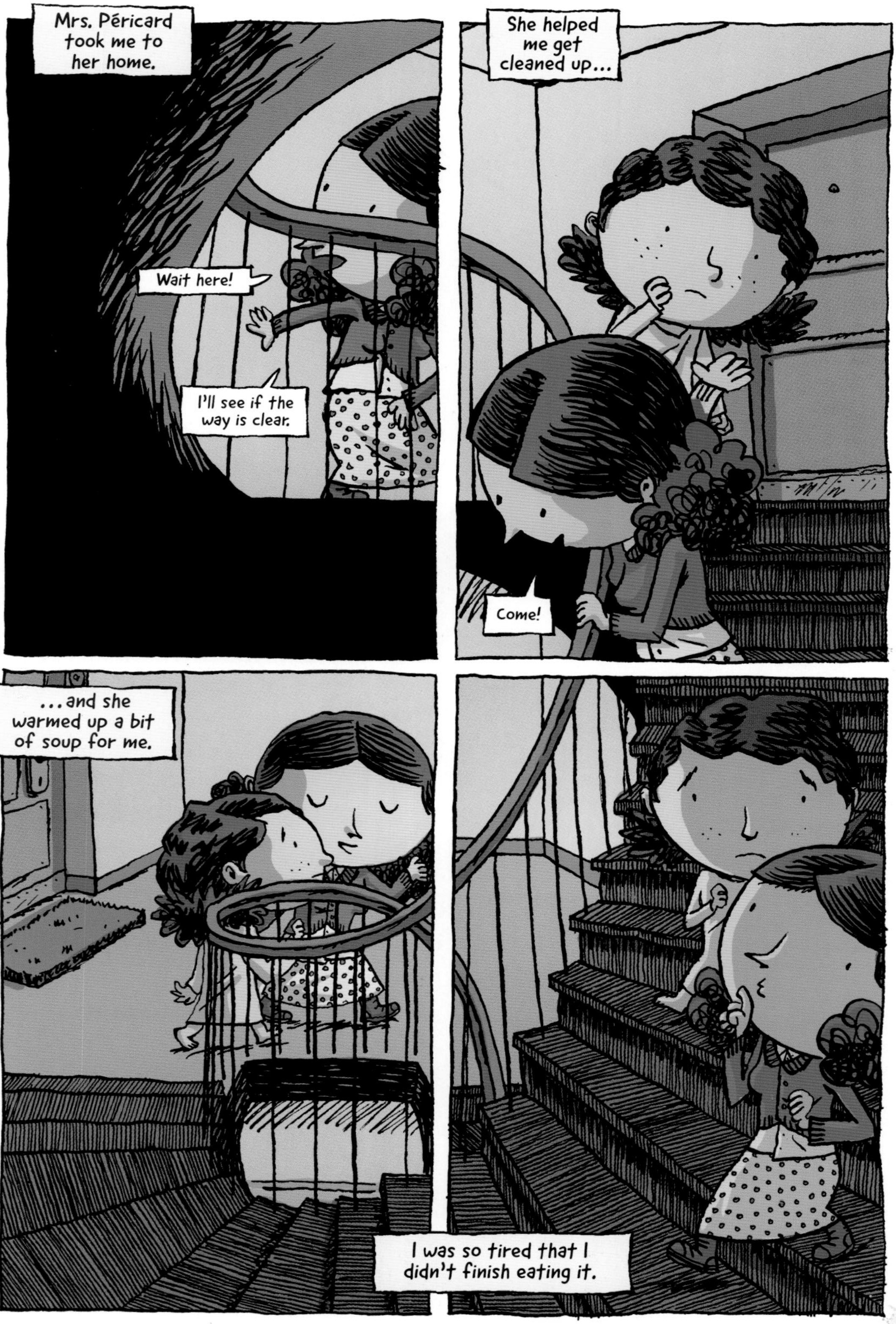
Mrs. Péricard took me to her home.
Wait here!
I'll see if the way is clear.
She helped me get cleaned up...
Come!
...and she warmed up a bit of soup for me.
I was so tired that I didn't finish eating it.

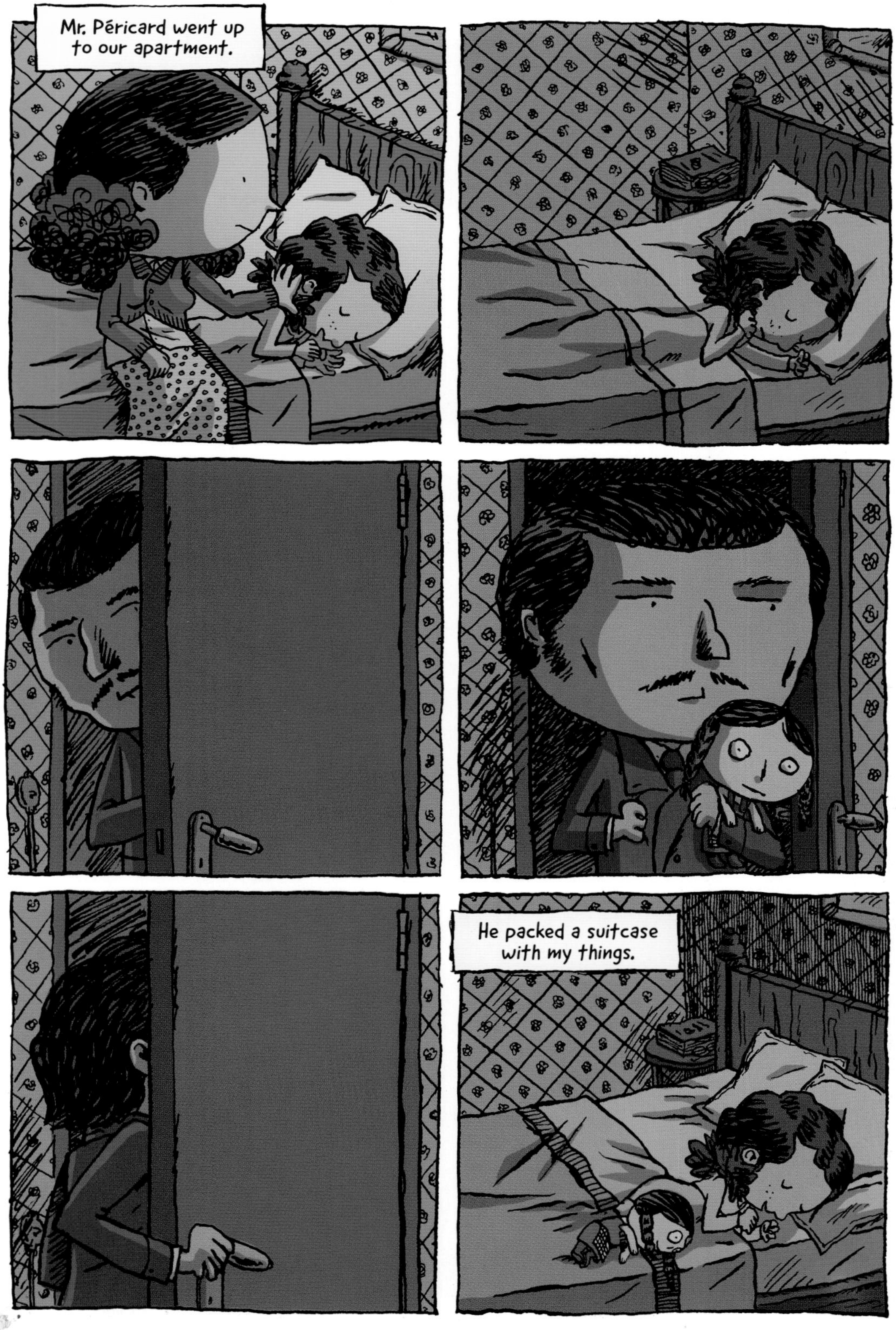
Mr. Péricard went up
to our apartment.
He packed a suitcase
with my things.

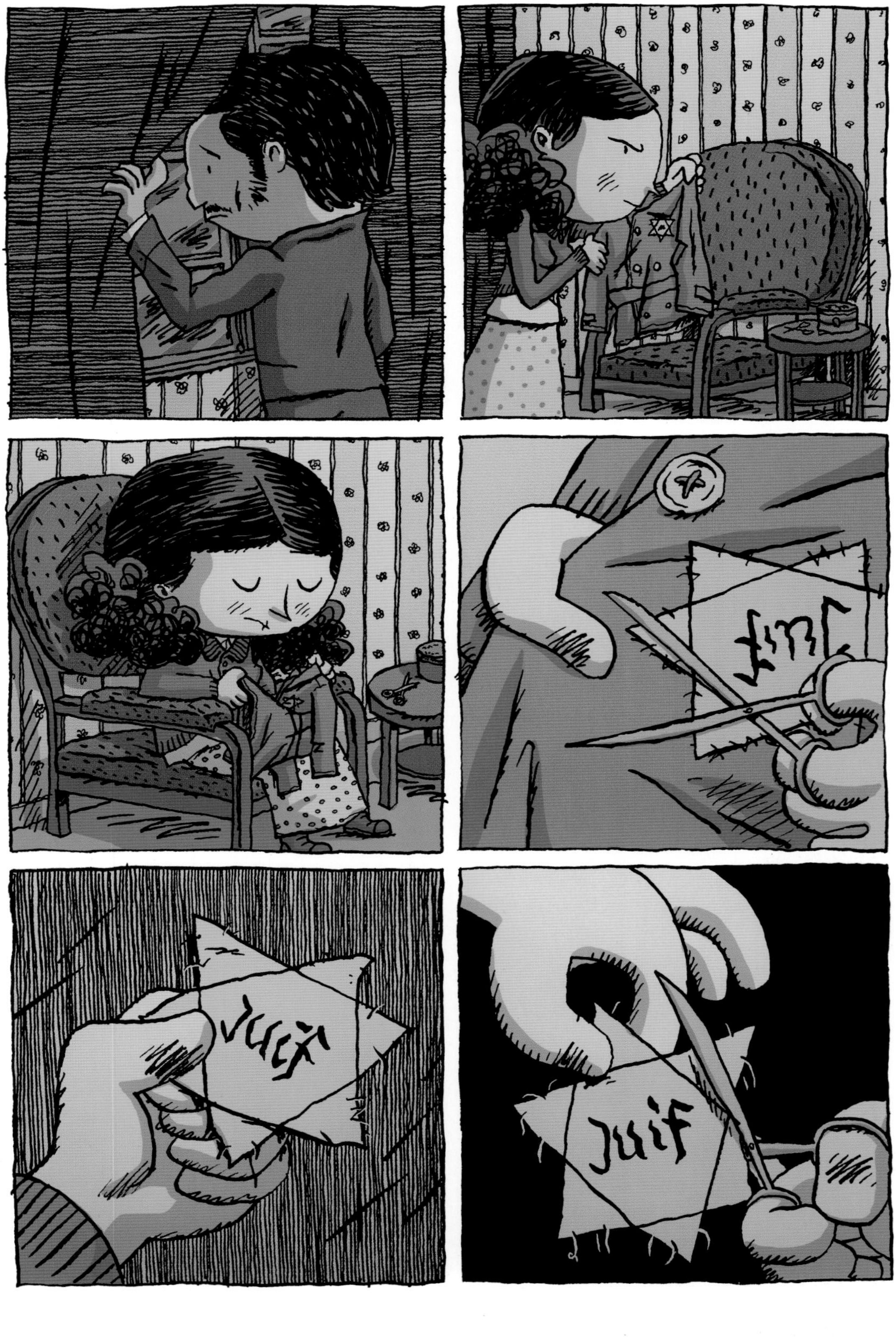
Juif
Juif

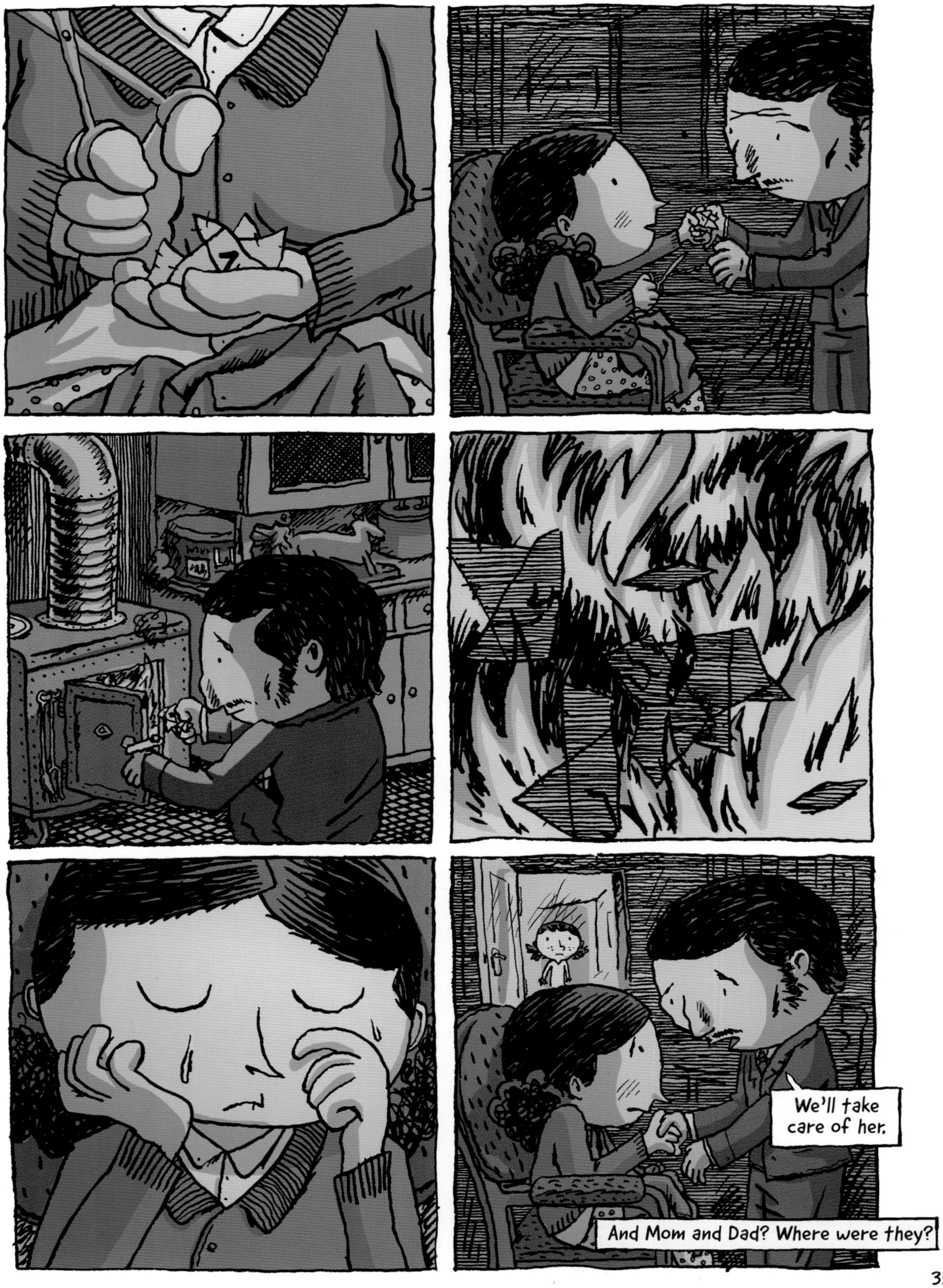
We'll take care of her.
And Mom and Dad? Where were they?

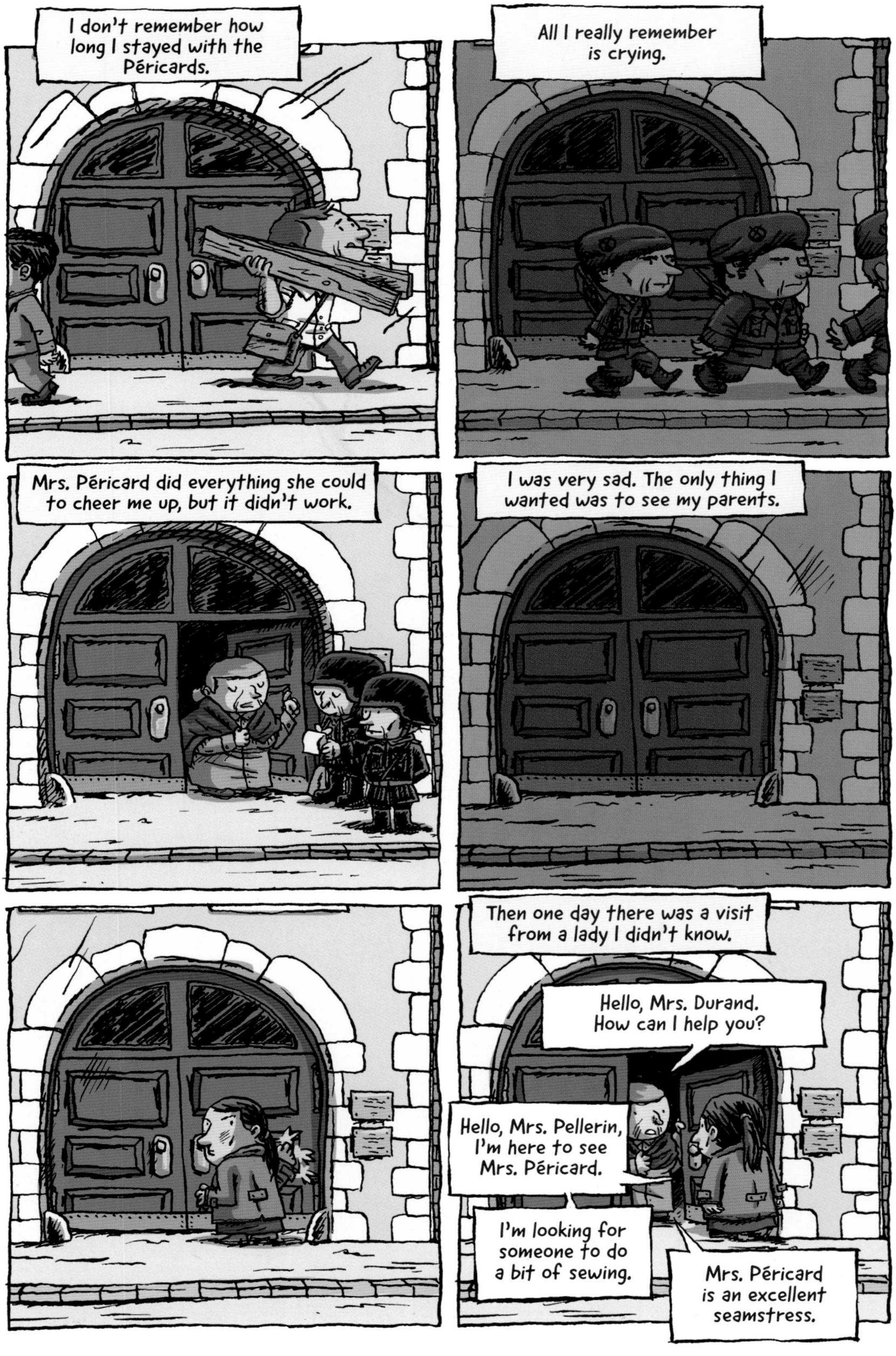
I don't remember how long I stayed with the Péricards.
All I really remember is crying.
Mrs. Péricard did everything she could to cheer me up, but it didn't work.
I was very sad. The only thing I wanted was to see my parents.
Then one day there was a visit from a lady I didn't know.
Hello, Mrs. Durand. How can I help you?
Hello, Mrs. Pellerin, I'm here to see Mrs. Péricard.
I'm looking for someone to do a bit of sewing.
Mrs. Péricard is an excellent seamstress.

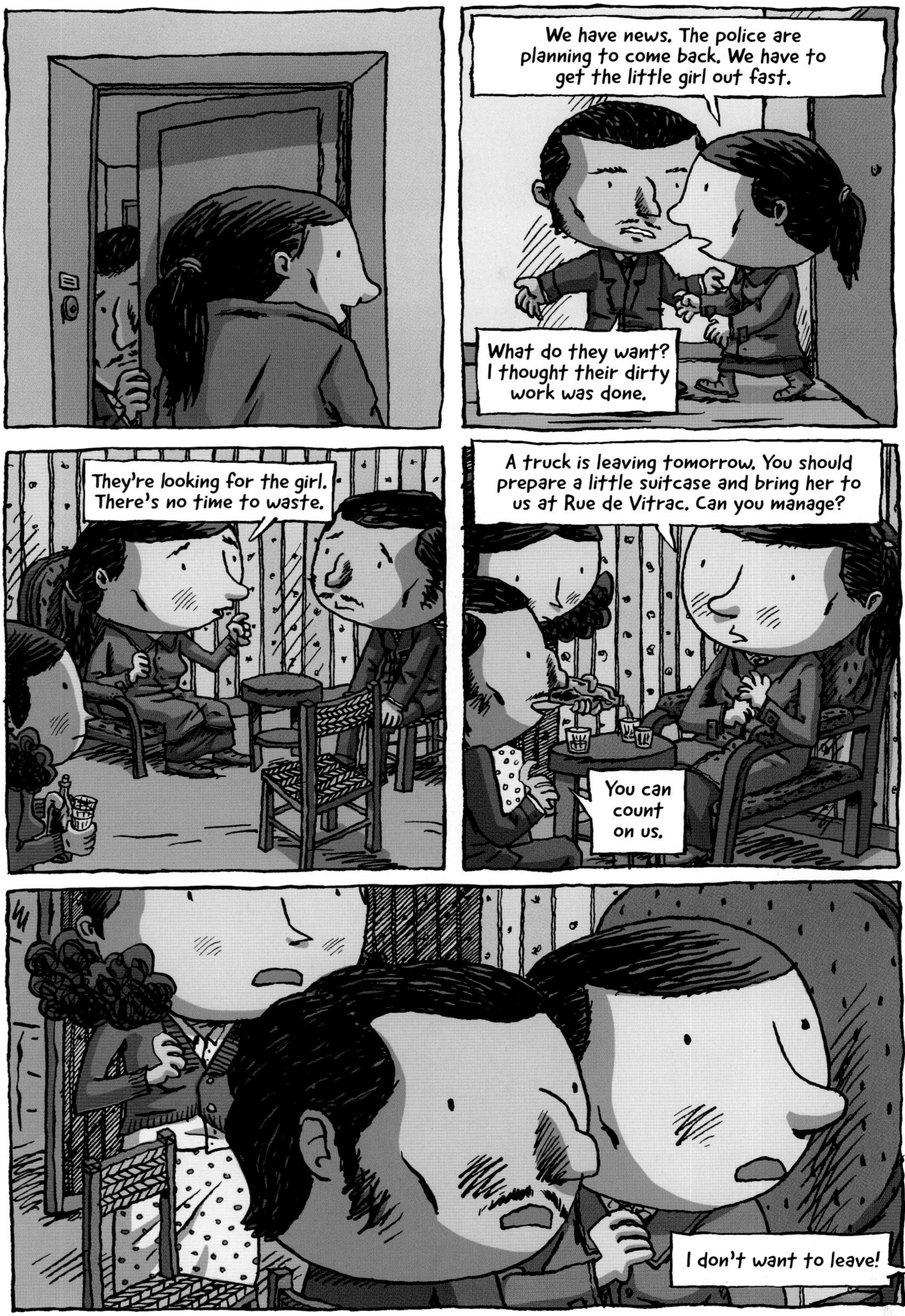
We have news. The police are planning to come back. We have to get the little girl out fast.
What do they want? I thought their dirty work was done.
They're looking for the girl. There's no time to waste.
A truck is leaving tomorrow. You should prepare a little suitcase and bring her to us at Rue de Vitrac. Can you manage?
You can count on us.
I don't want to leave!

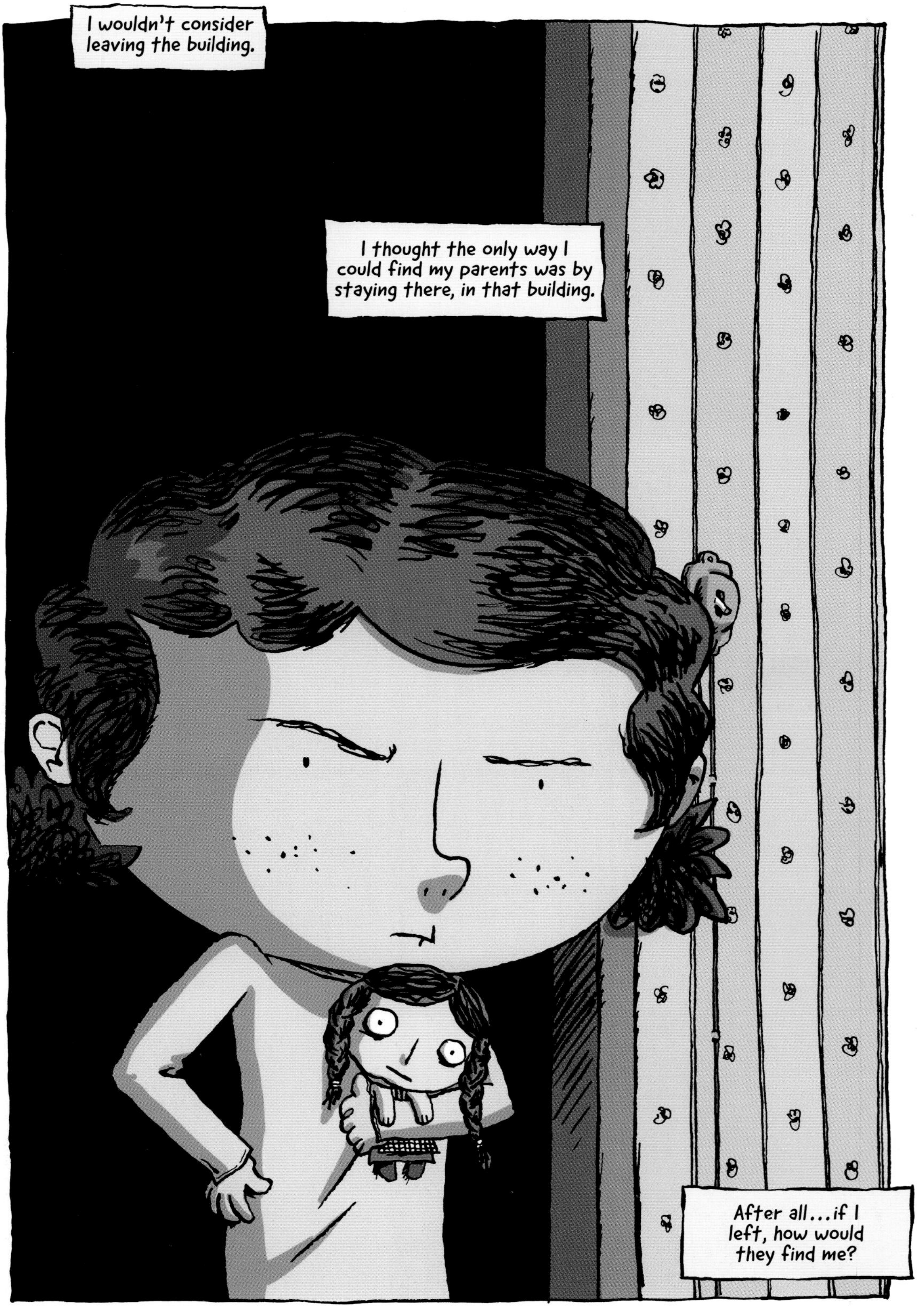
I wouldn't consider leaving the building.
I thought the only way I could find my parents was by staying there, in that building.
After all...if I left, how would they find me?

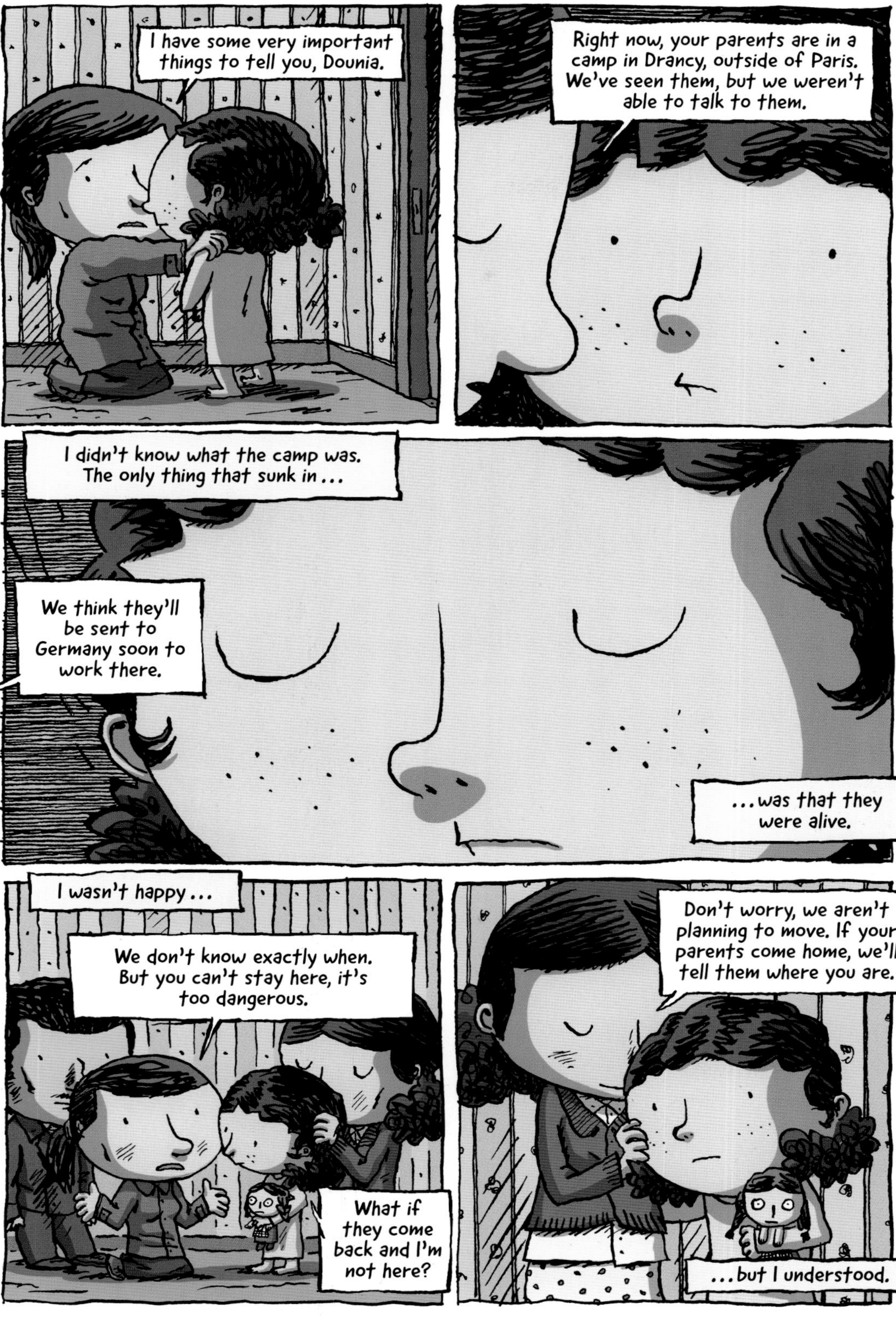
I have some very important things to tell you, Dounia.
Right now, your parents are in a camp in Drancy, outside of Paris. We've seen them, but we weren't able to talk to them.
I didn't know what the camp was. The only thing that sunk in ...
We think they'll be sent to Germany soon to work there.
... was that they were alive.
I wasn't happy ...
We don't know exactly when. But you can't stay here, it's too dangerous.
What if they come back and I'm not here?
Don't worry, we aren't planning to move. If your parents come home, we'll tell them where you are.
... but I understood.

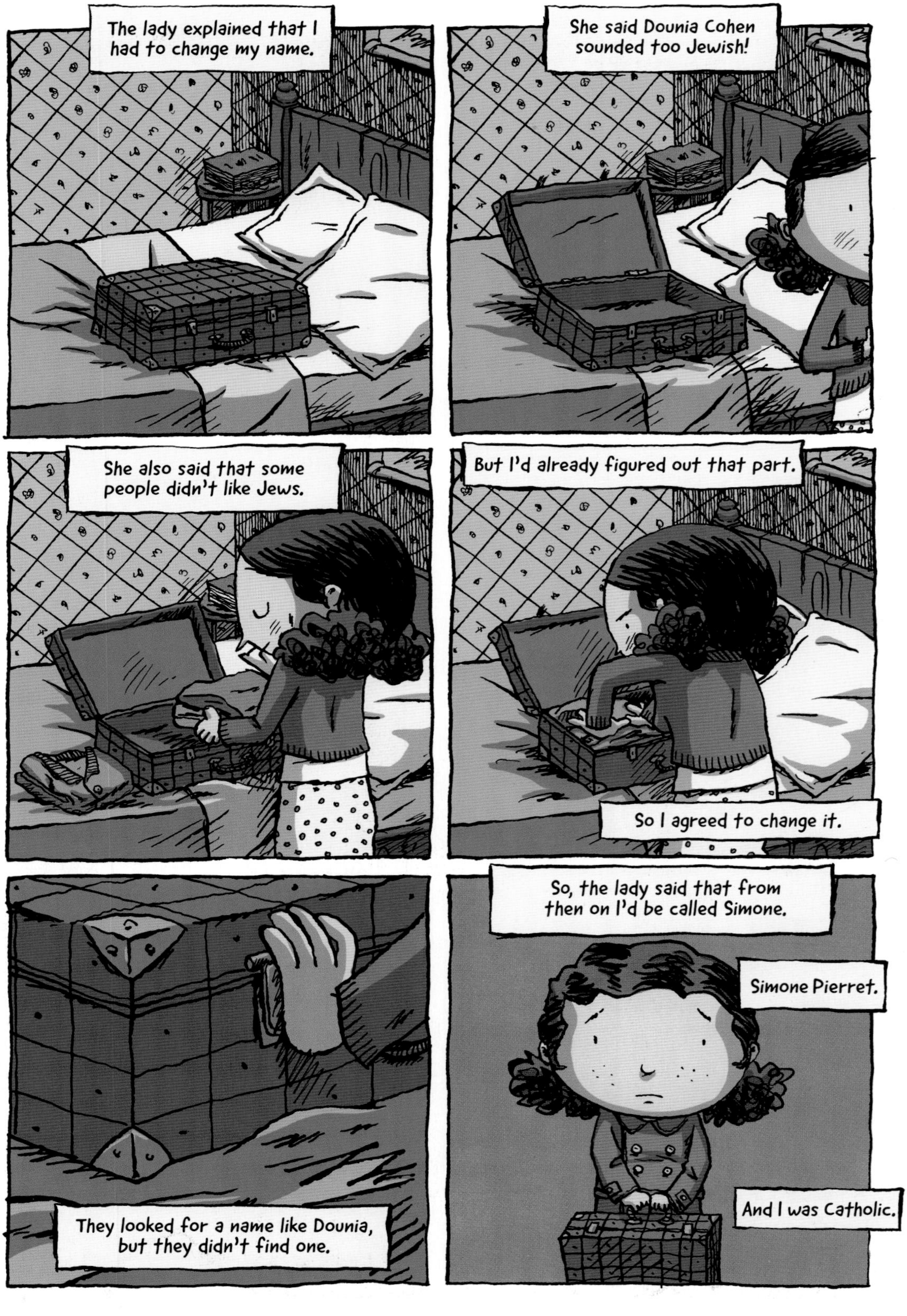
The lady explained that I had to change my name.
She said Dounia Cohen sounded too Jewish!
She also said that some people didn't like Jews.
But I'd already figured out that part.
So I agreed to change it.
They looked for a name like Dounia, but they didn't find one.
So, the lady said that from then on I'd be called Simone.
Simone Pierret.
And I was Catholic.

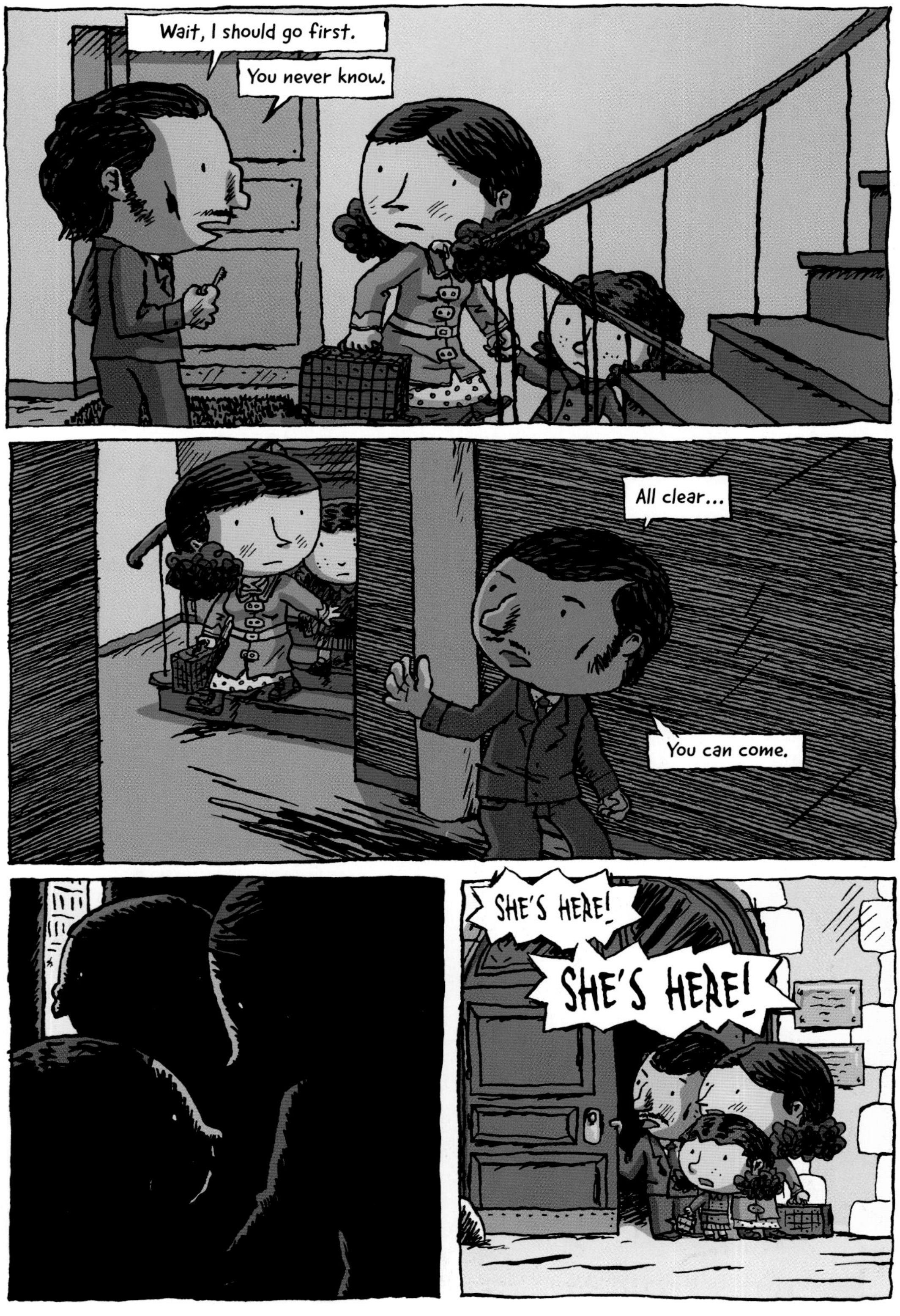
Wait, I should go first.
You never know.
All clear...
You can come.
SHE'S HERE!
SHE'S HERE!

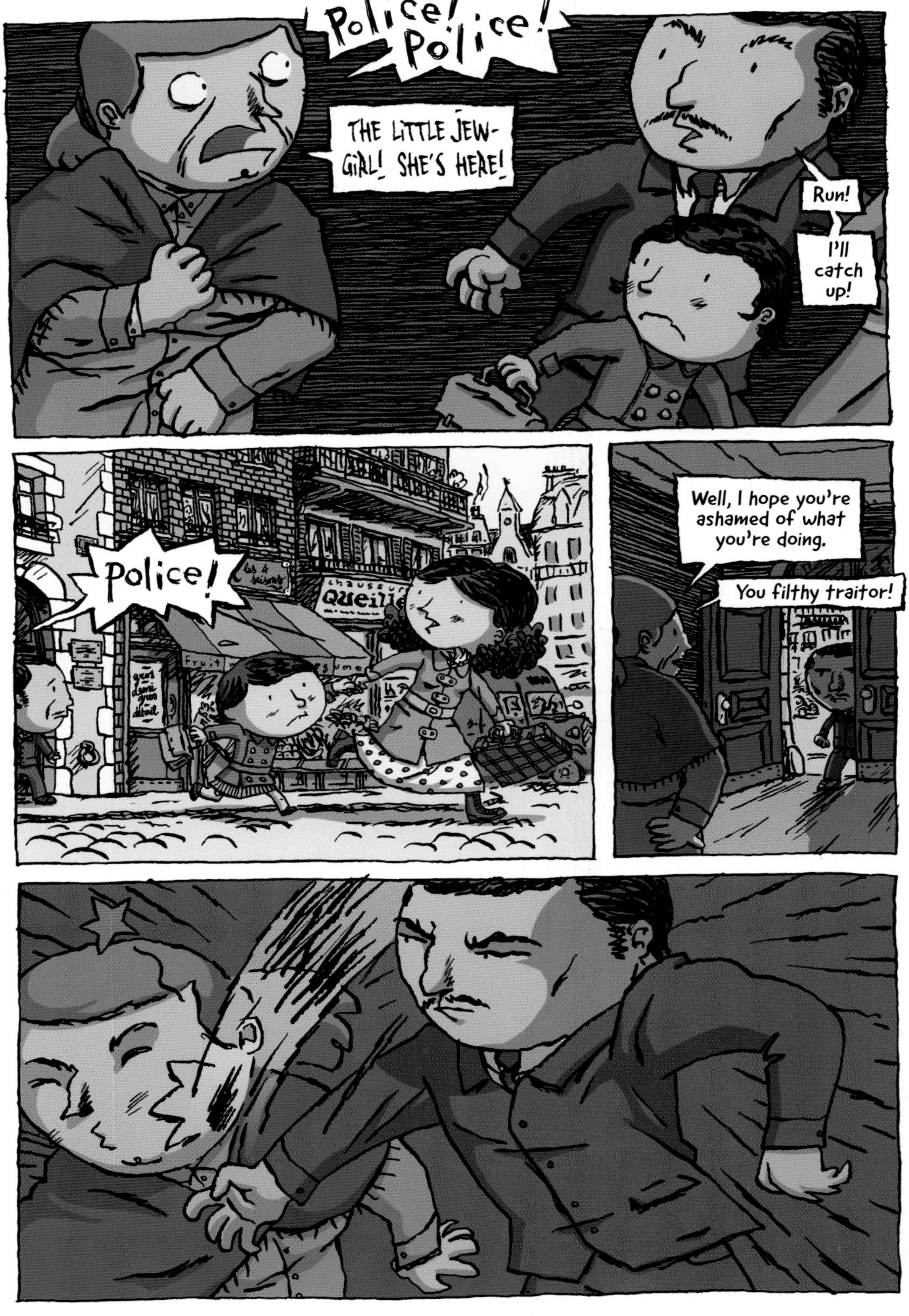
Police! Police!
THE LITTLE JEW-GIRL! SHE'S HERE!
Run!
I'll catch up!
Police!
Well, I hope you're ashamed of what you're doing.
You filthy traitor!

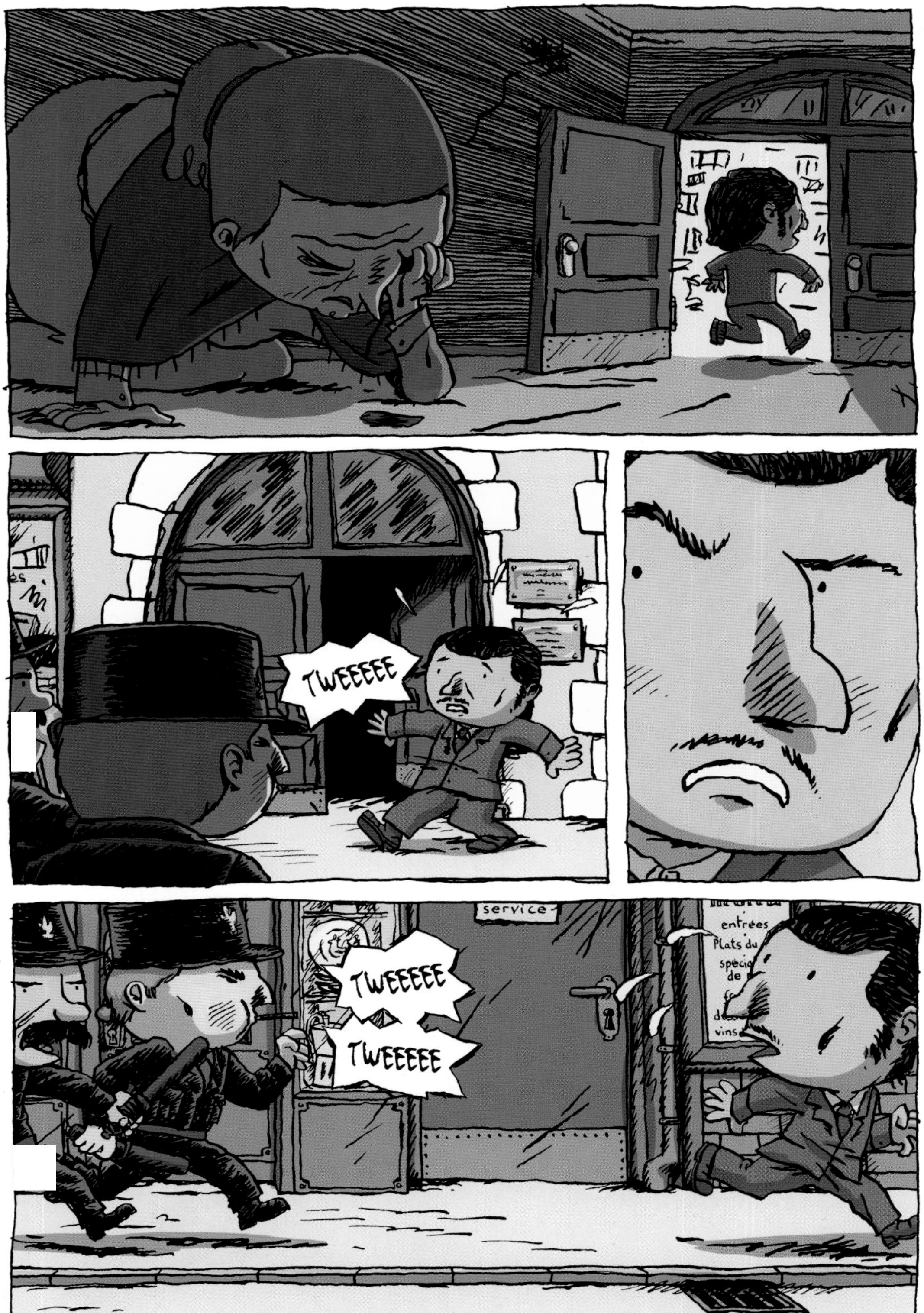
TWEEEEE
service
entrées
Plats du
TWEEEEE
TWEEEEE

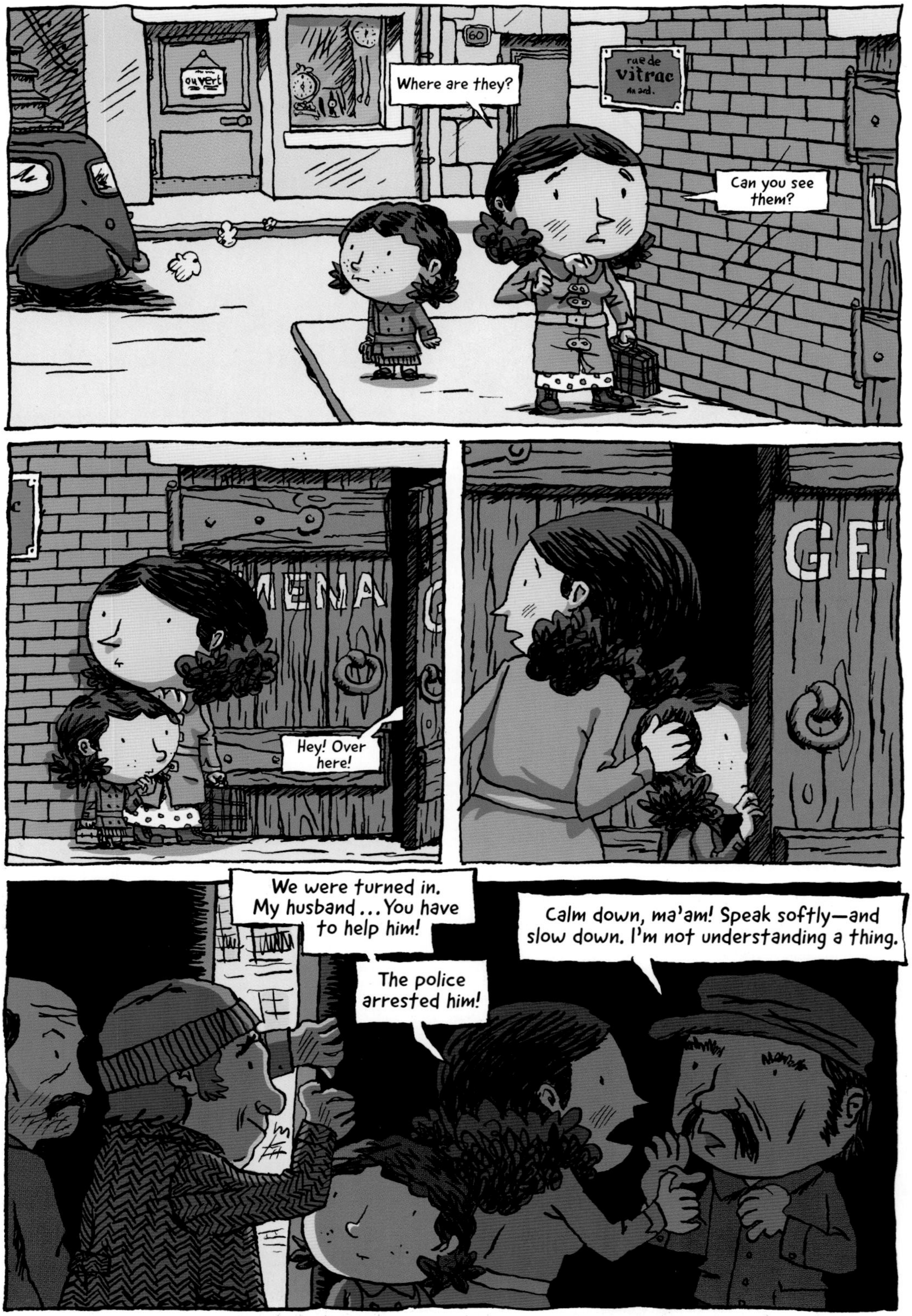
ouvert
rue de vitrac
Where are they?
Can you see them?
MENA
Hey! Over here!
GE
We were turned in. My husband... You have to help him!
The police arrested him!
Calm down, ma'am! Speak softly—and slow down. I'm not understanding a thing.

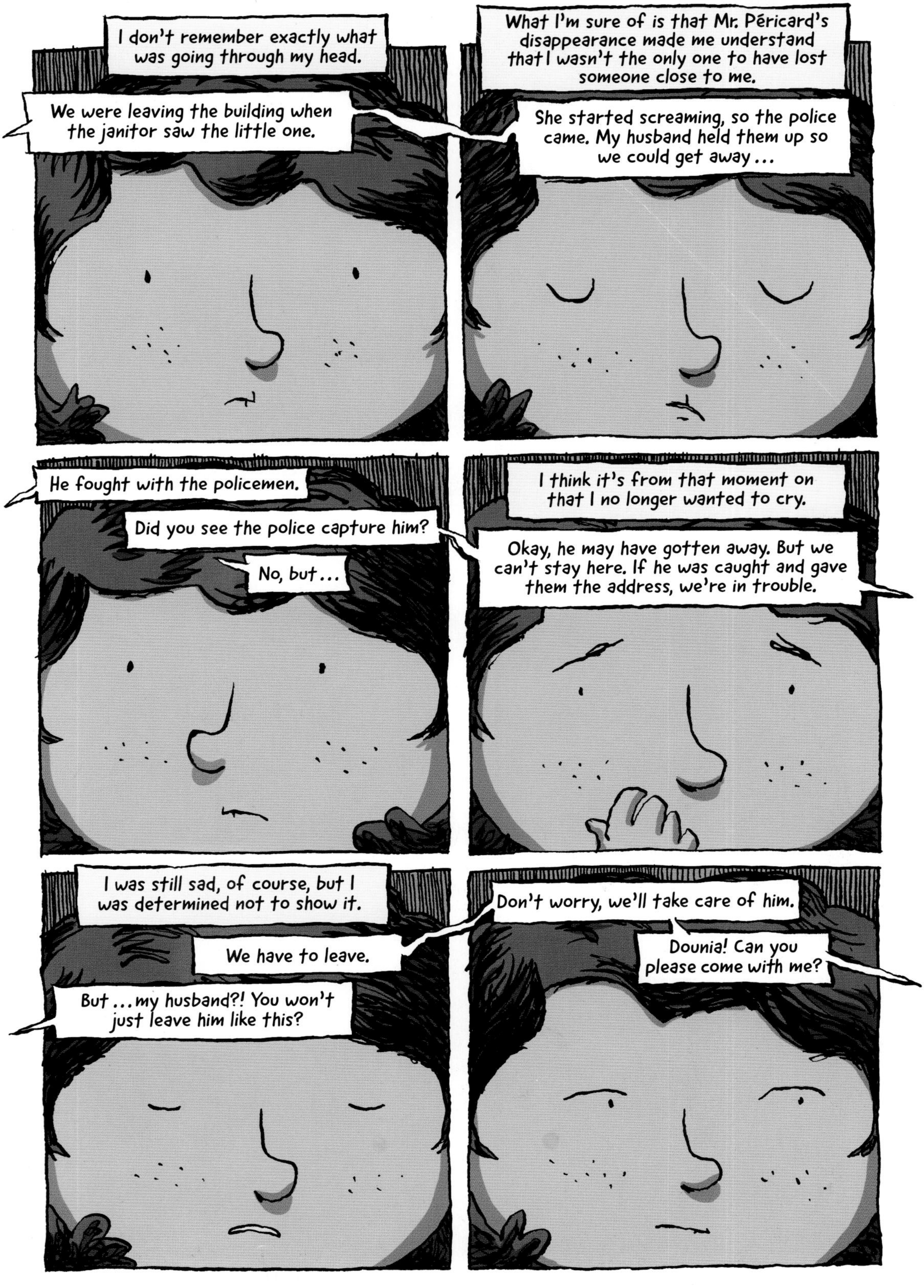
I don't remember exactly what was going through my head.
We were leaving the building when the janitor saw the little one.
What I'm sure of is that Mr. Péricard's disappearance made me understand that I wasn't the only one to have lost someone close to me.
She started screaming, so the police came. My husband held them up so we could get away...
He fought with the policemen.
Did you see the police capture him?
No, but...
I think it's from that moment on that I no longer wanted to cry.
Okay, he may have gotten away. But we can't stay here. If he was caught and gave them the address, we're in trouble.
I was still sad, of course, but I was determined not to show it.
We have to leave.
But... my husband?! You won't just leave him like this?
Don't worry, we'll take care of him.
Dounia! Can you please come with me?

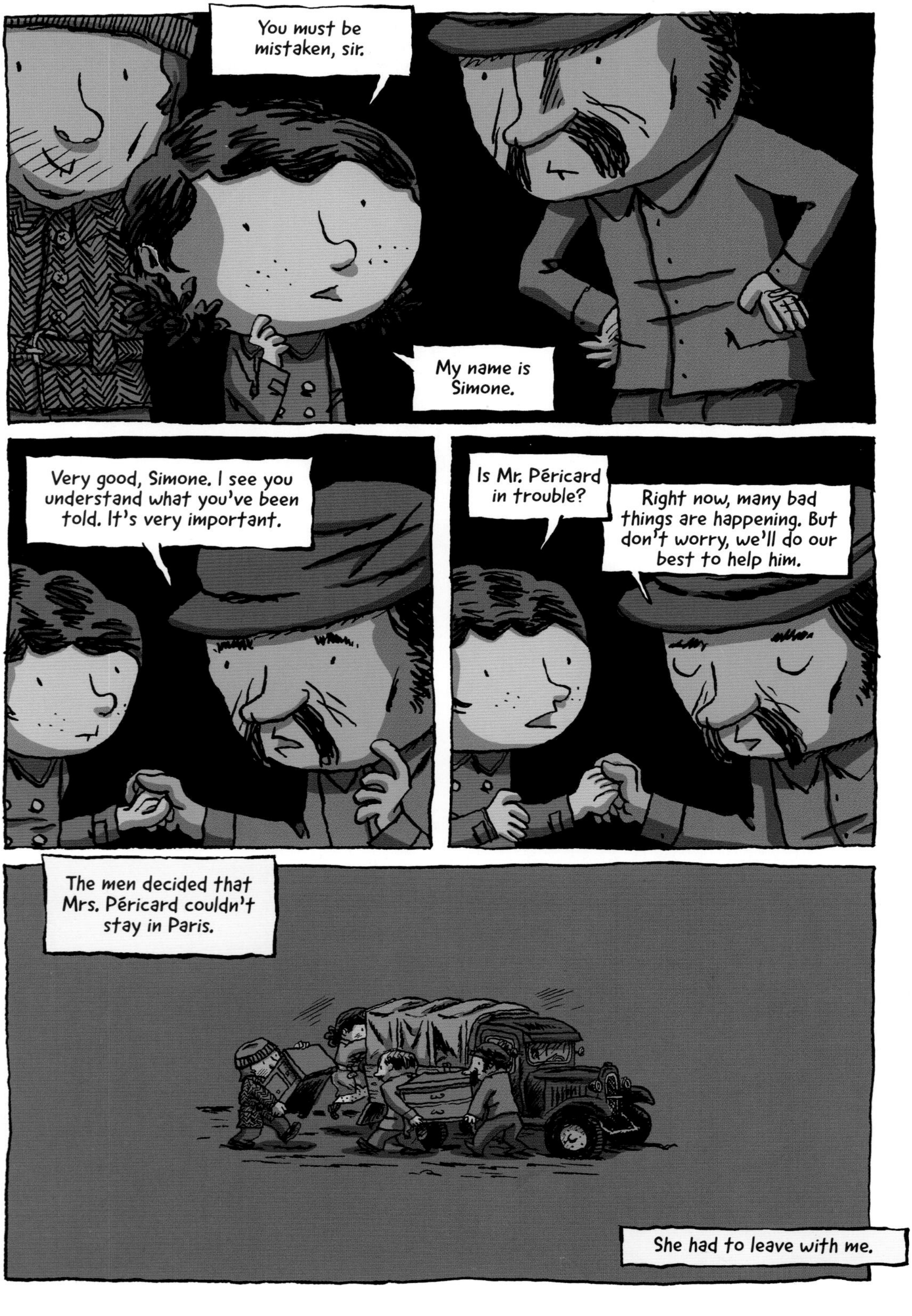
You must be mistaken, sir.
My name is Simone.
Very good, Simone. I see you understand what you've been told. It's very important.
Is Mr. Péricard in trouble?
Right now, many bad things are happening. But don't worry, we'll do our best to help him.
The men decided that Mrs. Péricard couldn't stay in Paris.
She had to leave with me.

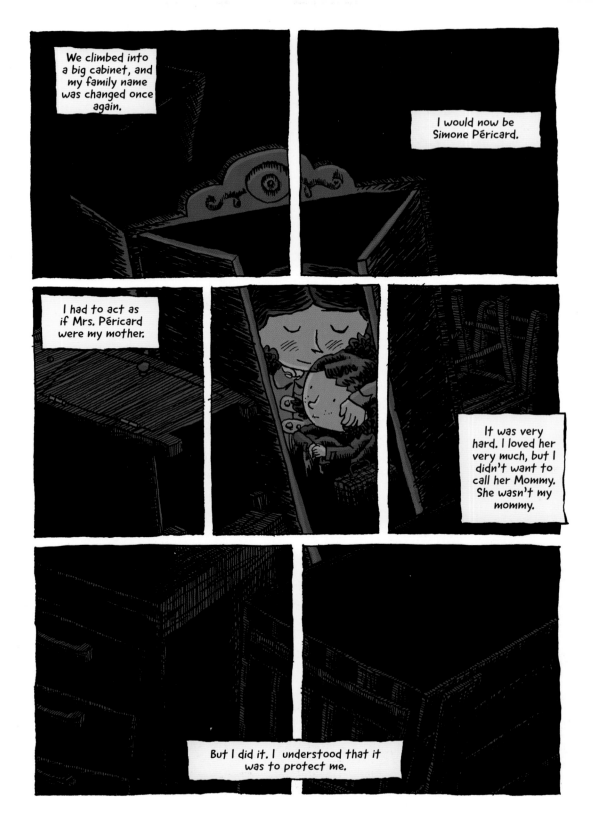

We climbed into a big cabinet, and my family name was changed once again.

I would now be Simone Péricard.

I had to act as if Mrs. Péricard were my mother.

It was very hard. I loved her very much, but I didn't want to call her Mommy. She wasn't my mommy.

But I did it. I understood that it was to protect me.

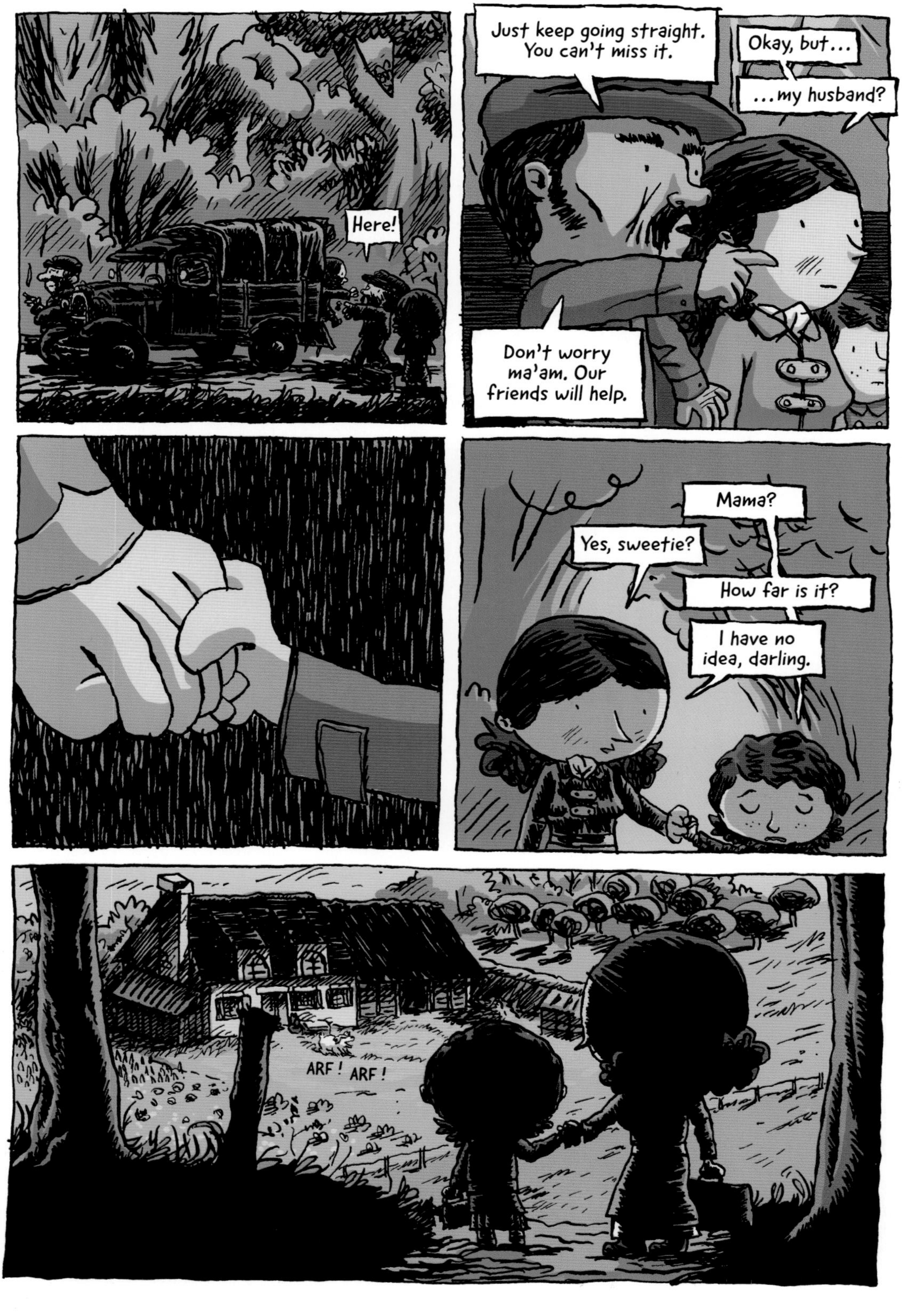
Here!
Just keep going straight. You can't miss it.
Okay, but...
...my husband?
Don't worry ma'am. Our friends will help.
Mama?
Yes, sweetie?
How far is it?
I have no idea, darling.
ARF! ARF!

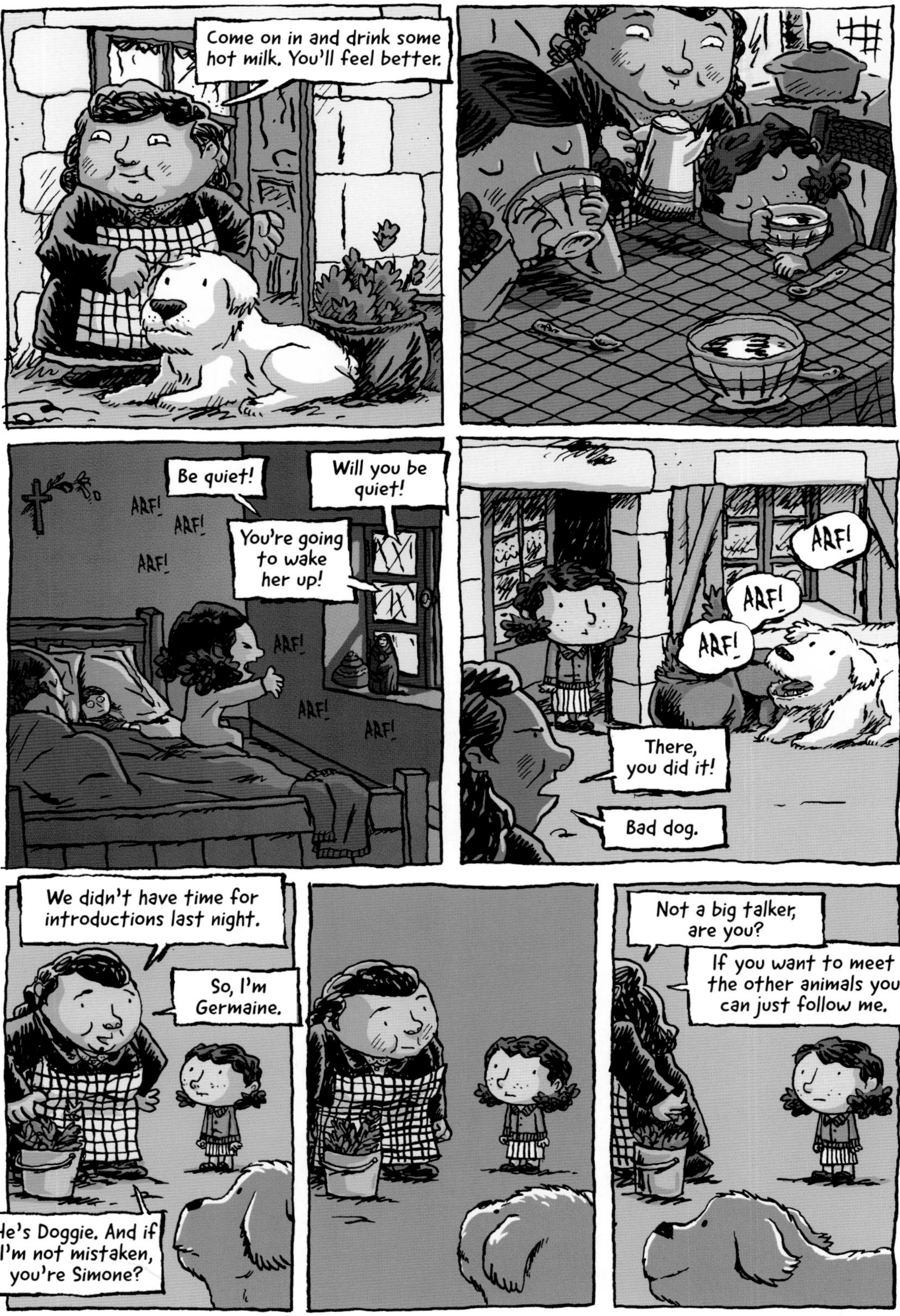
Come on in and drink some hot milk. You'll feel better.
Be quiet!
ARF!
ARF!
ARF!
Will you be quiet!
You're going to wake her up!
ARF!
ARF!
ARF!
ARF!
ARF!
ARF!
There, you did it!
Bad dog.
We didn't have time for introductions last night.
So, I'm Germaine.
He's Doggie. And if I'm not mistaken, you're Simone?
Not a big talker, are you?
If you want to meet the other animals you can just follow me.

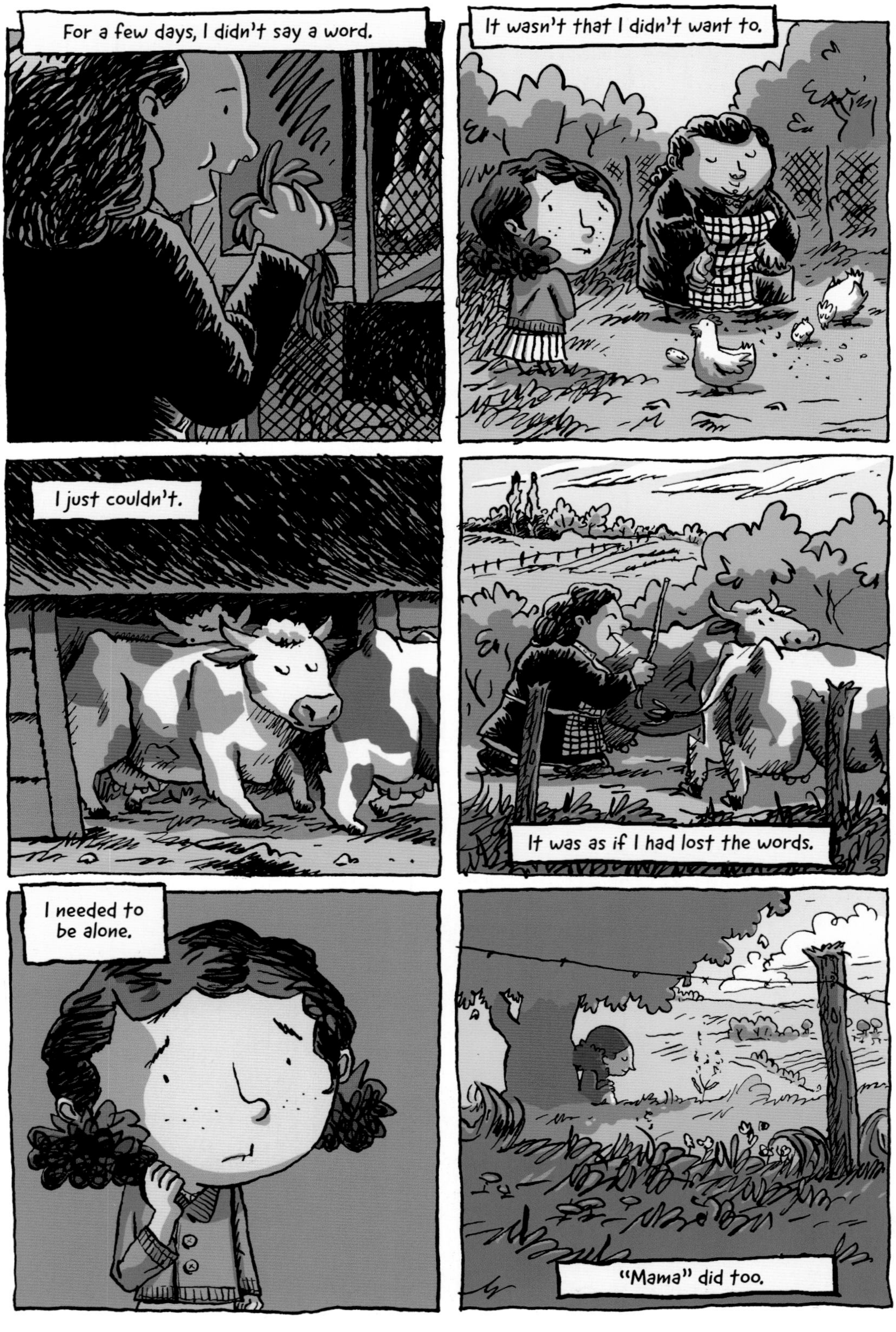
For a few days, I didn't say a word.
It wasn't that I didn't want to.
I just couldn't.
It was as if I had lost the words.
I needed to be alone.
"Mama" did too.

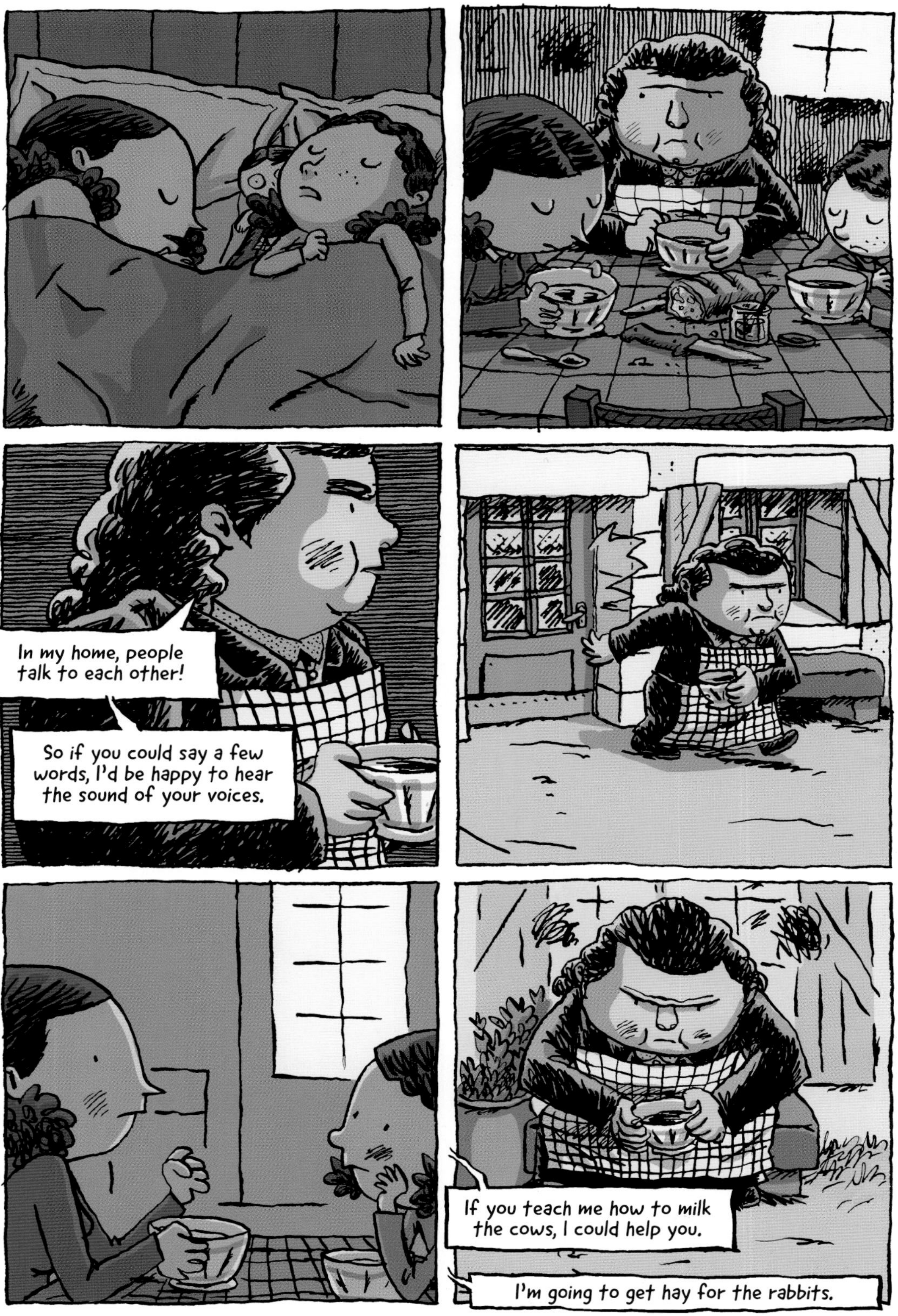
In my home, people talk to each other!
So if you could say a few words, I'd be happy to hear the sound of your voices.
If you teach me how to milk the cows, I could help you.
I'm going to get hay for the rabbits.

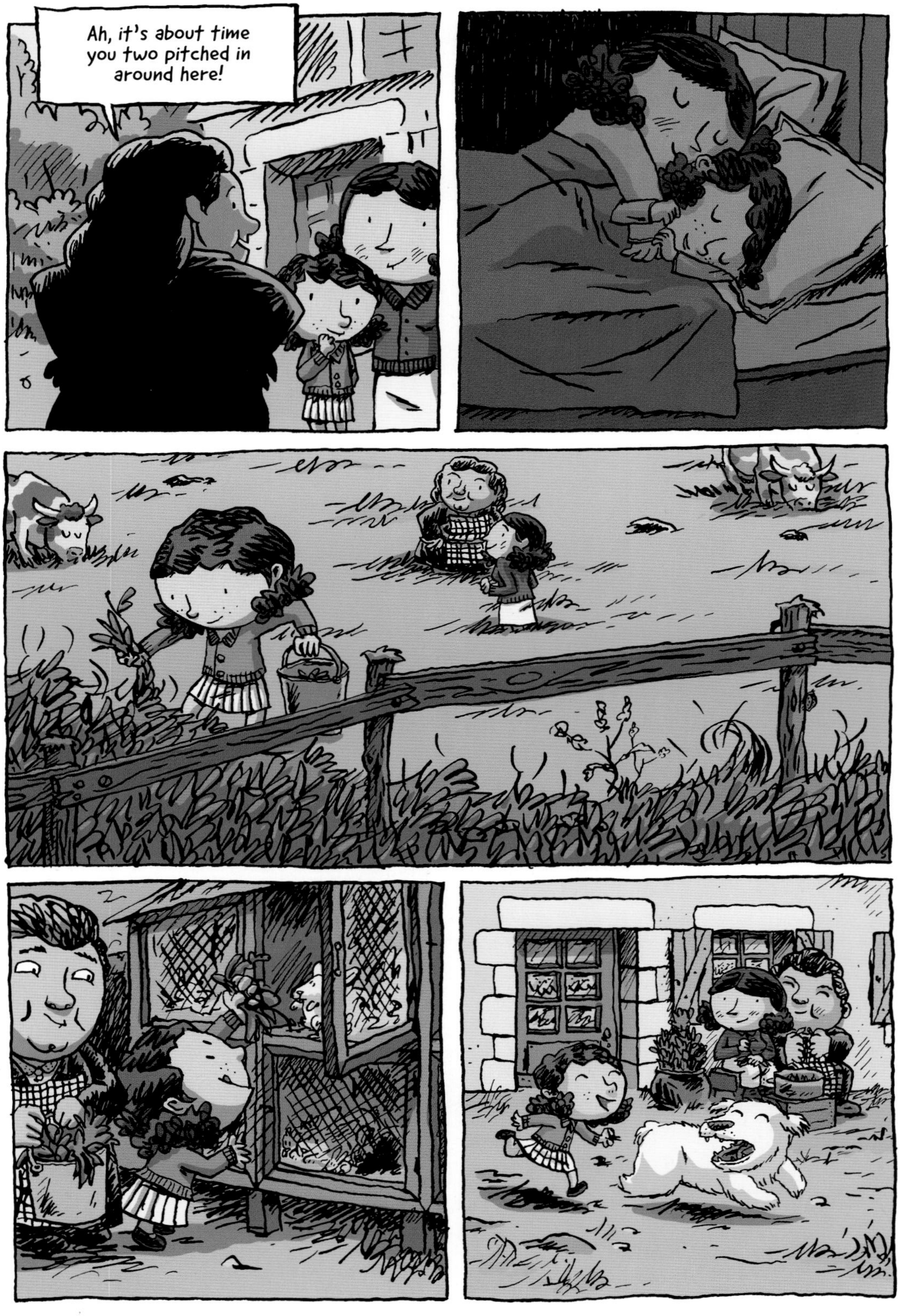
Ah, it's about time you two pitched in around here!

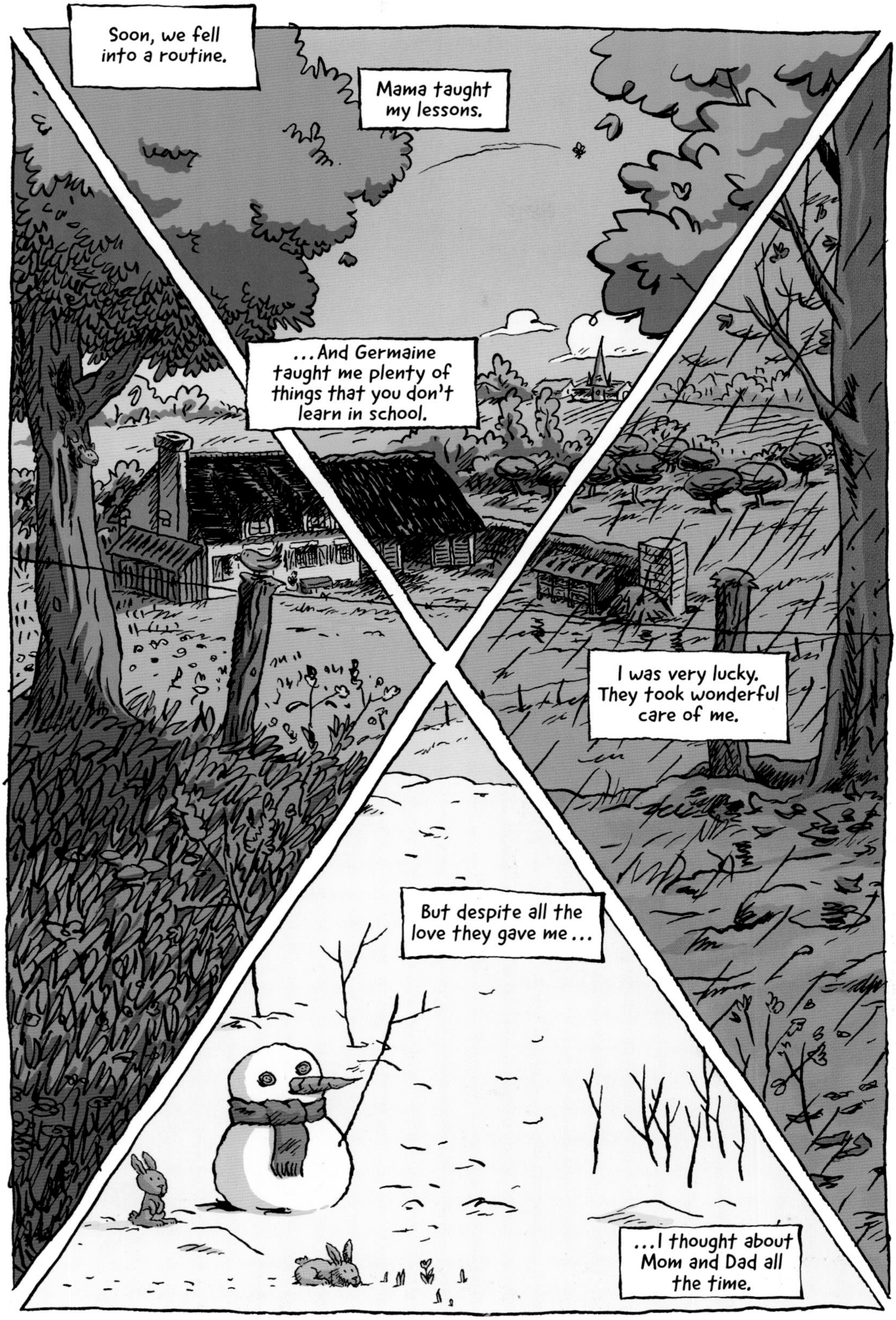
Soon, we fell into a routine.
Mama taught my lessons.
...And Germaine taught me plenty of things that you don't learn in school.
I was very lucky. They took wonderful care of me.
But despite all the love they gave me...
...I thought about Mom and Dad all the time.

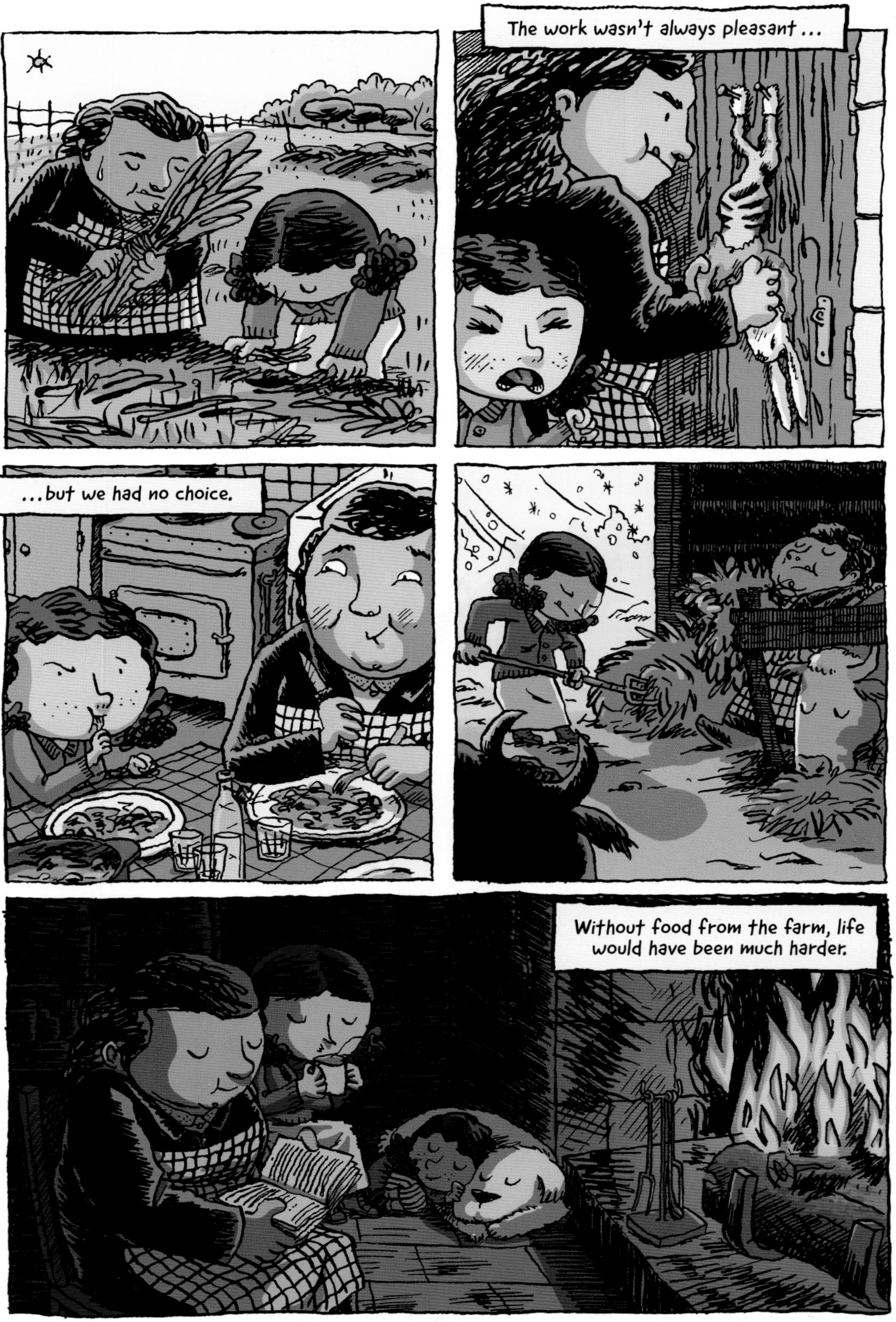
The work wasn't always pleasant . . .
. . . but we had no choice.
Without food from the farm, life would have been much harder.

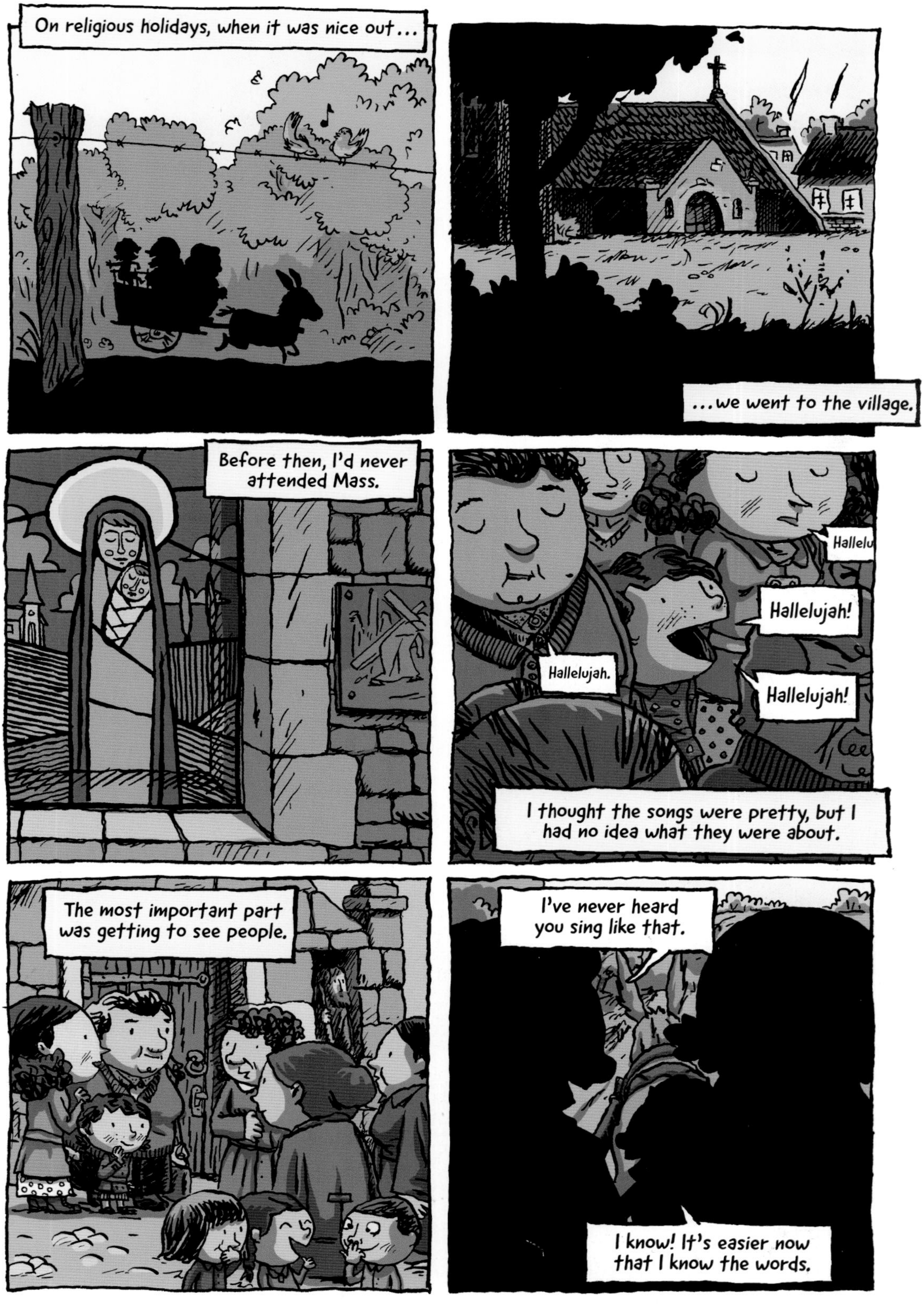
On religious holidays, when it was nice out...
...we went to the village.
Before then, I'd never attended Mass.
Hallelu
Hallelujah!
Hallelujah.
Hallelujah!
I thought the songs were pretty, but I had no idea what they were about.
The most important part was getting to see people.
I've never heard you sing like that.
I know! It's easier now that I know the words.

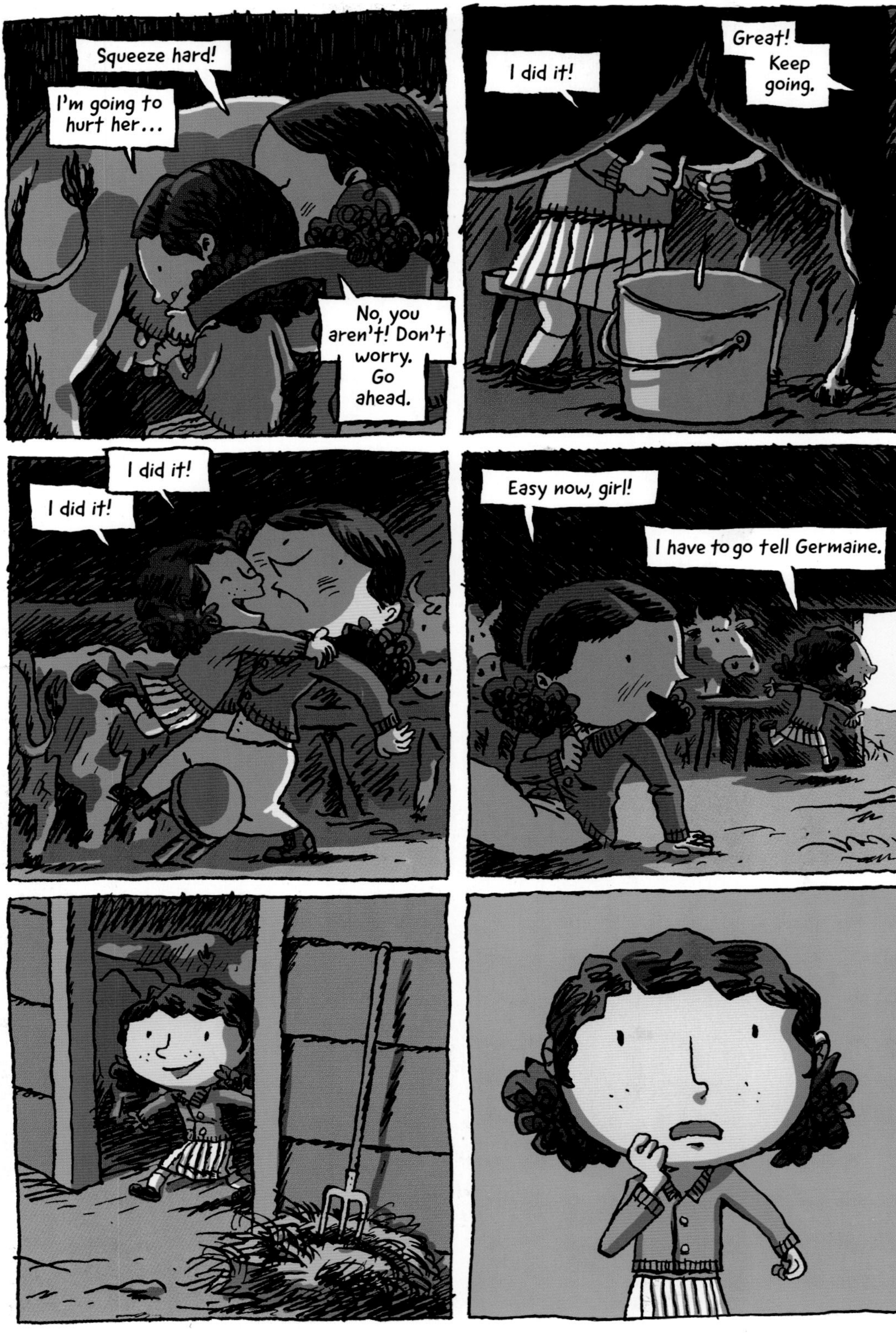
Squeeze hard!
I'm going to hurt her...
No, you aren't! Don't worry. Go ahead.
I did it!
Great!
Keep going.
I did it!
I did it!
Easy now, girl!
I have to go tell Germaine.

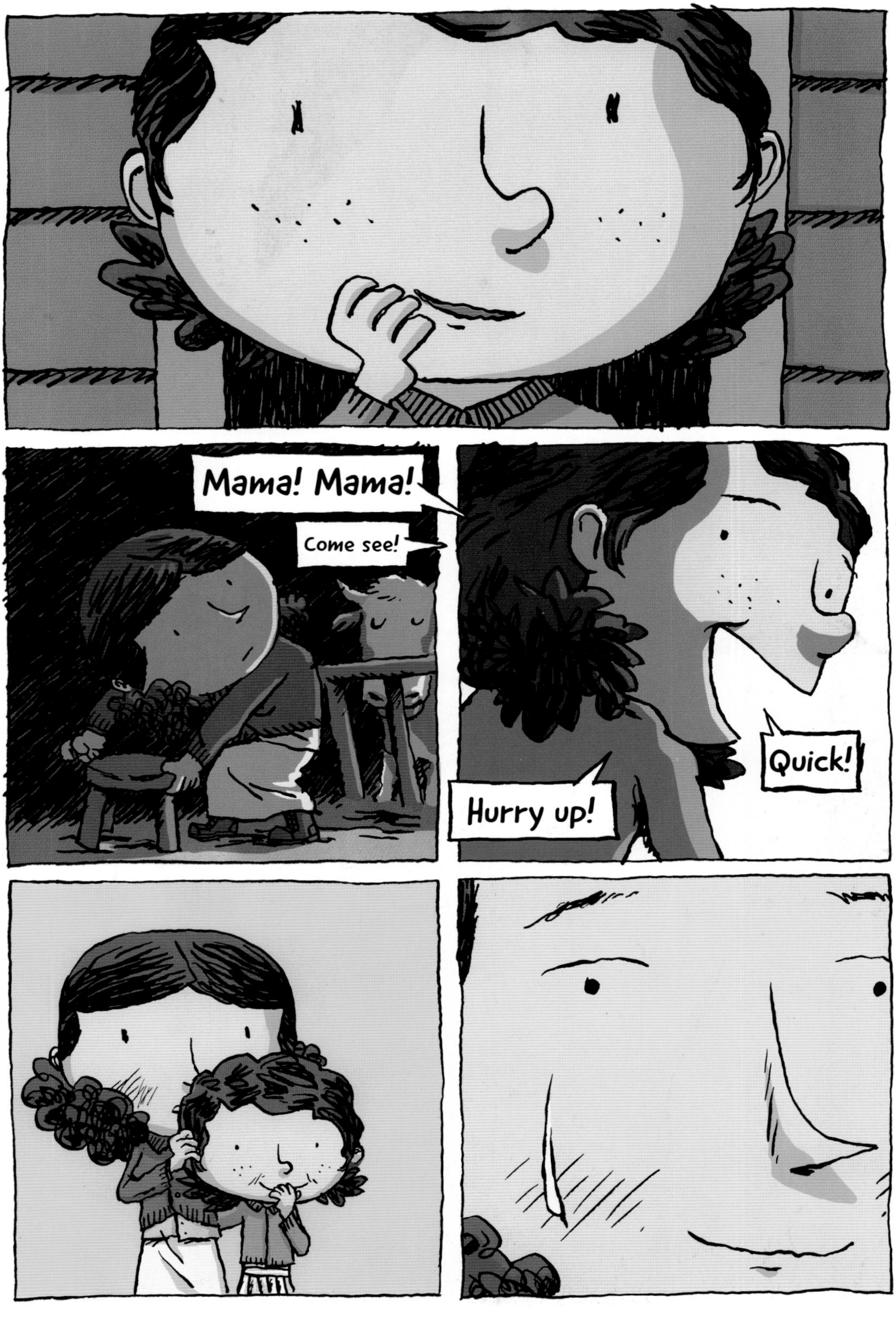
Mama! Mama!
Come see!
Quick!
Hurry up!

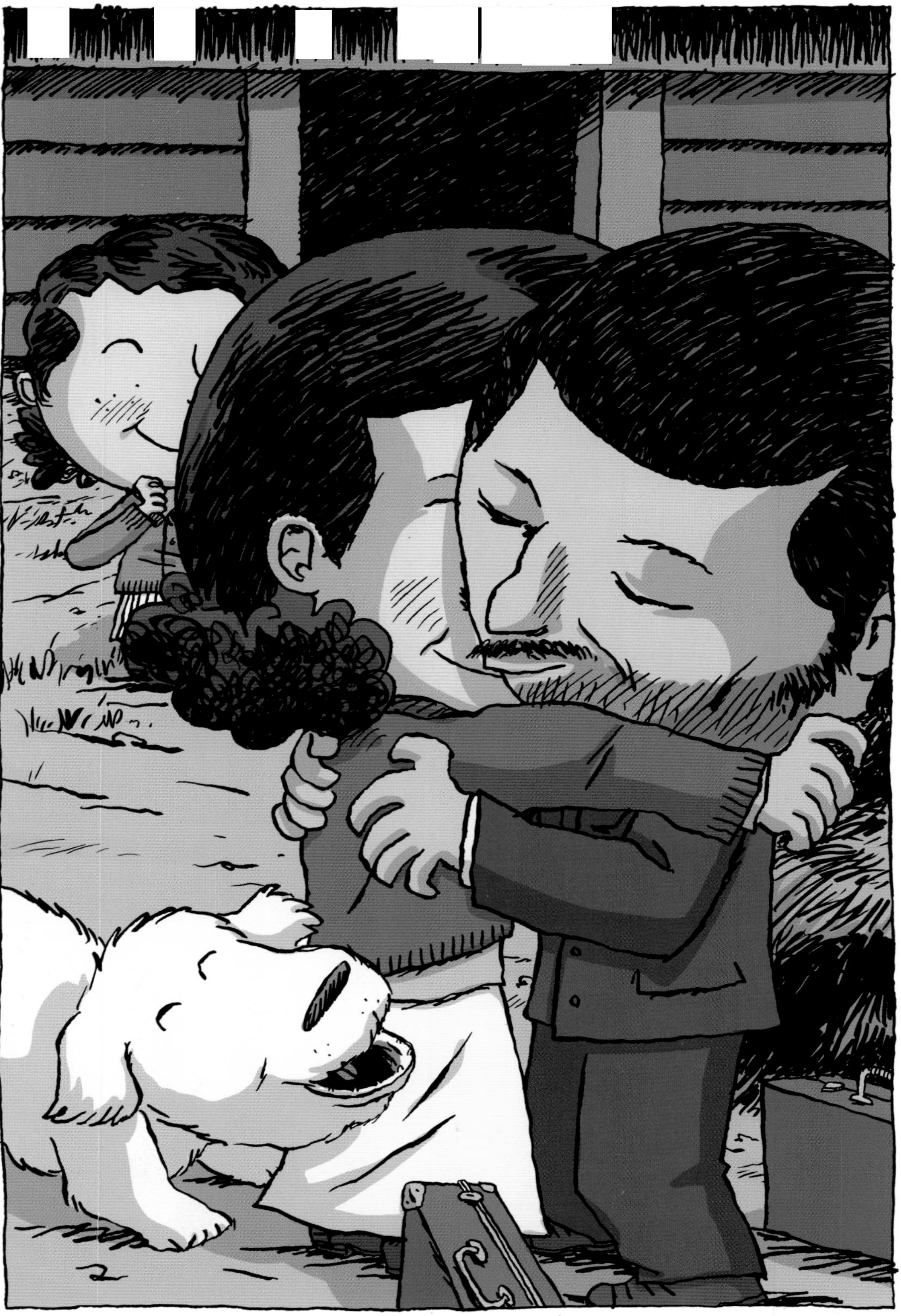

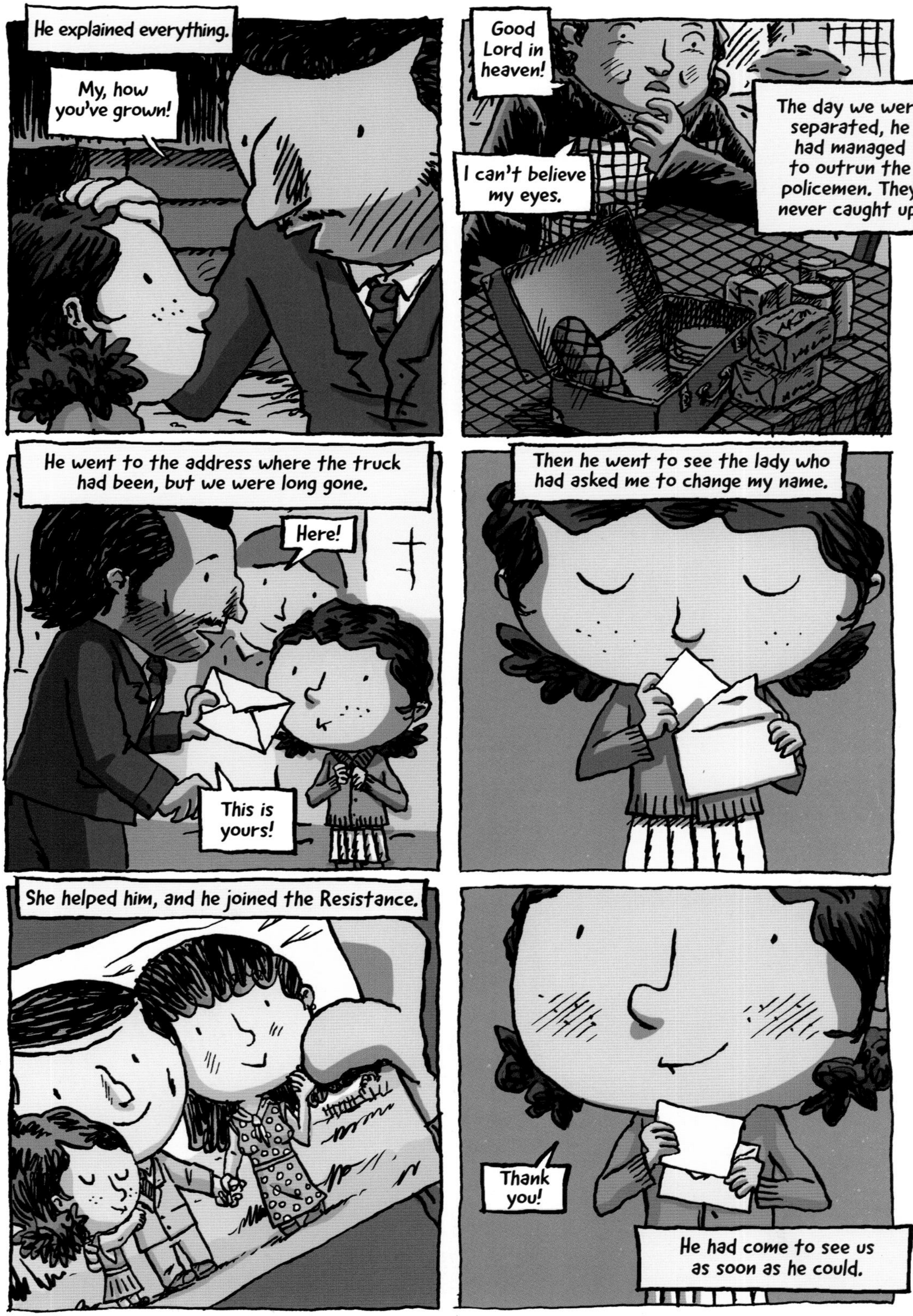
He explained everything.
My, how you've grown!
Good Lord in heaven!
I can't believe my eyes.
The day we were separated, he had managed to outrun the policemen. They never caught up.
He went to the address where the truck had been, but we were long gone.
Here!
This is yours!
Then he went to see the lady who had asked me to change my name.
She helped him, and he joined the Resistance.
Thank you!
He had come to see us as soon as he could.

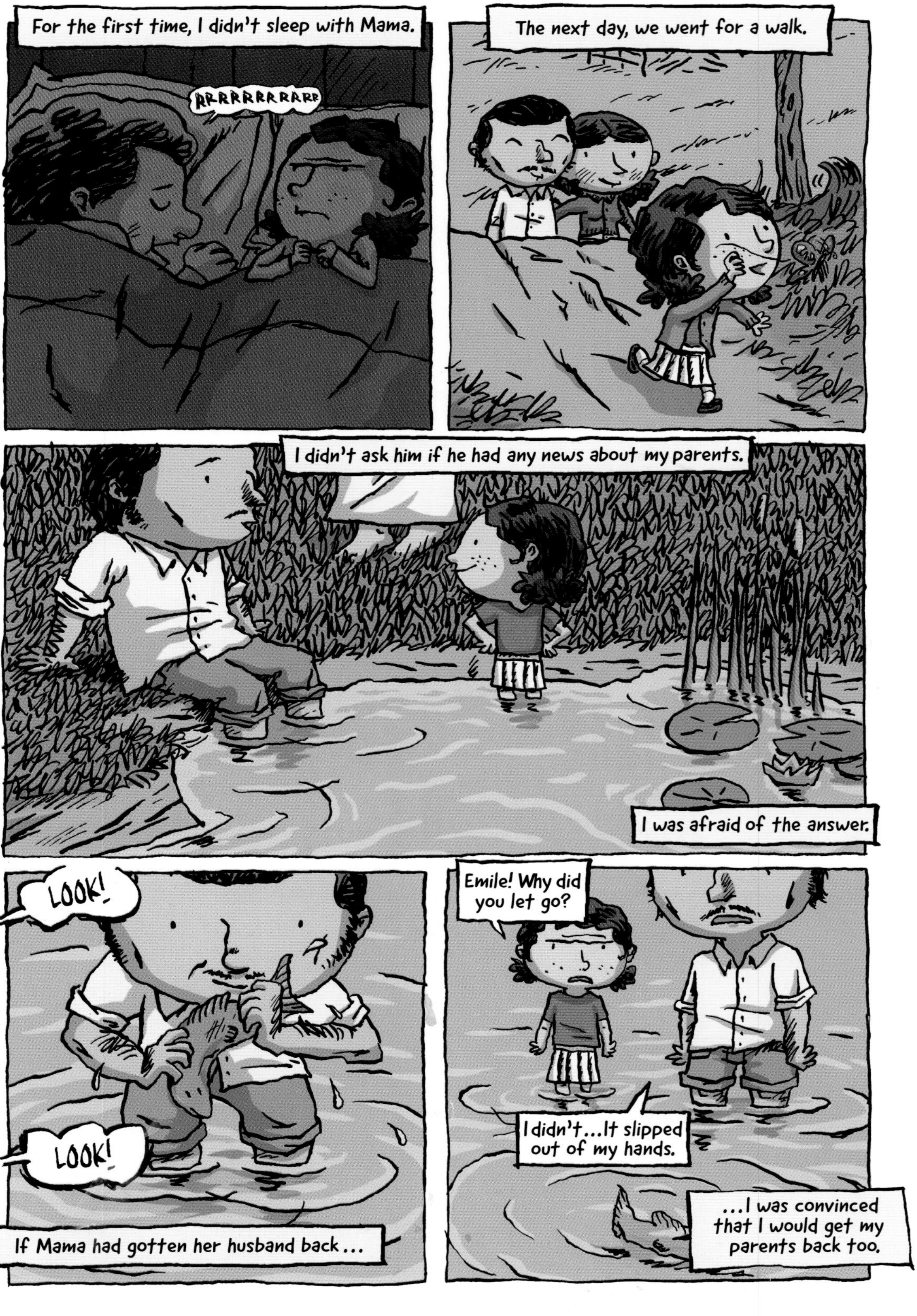
For the first time, I didn't sleep with Mama.
RRRRRRRRRRRR
The next day, we went for a walk.
I didn't ask him if he had any news about my parents.
I was afraid of the answer.
LOOK!
LOOK!
If Mama had gotten her husband back...
Emile! Why did you let go?
I didn't...It slipped out of my hands.
...I was convinced that I would get my parents back too.

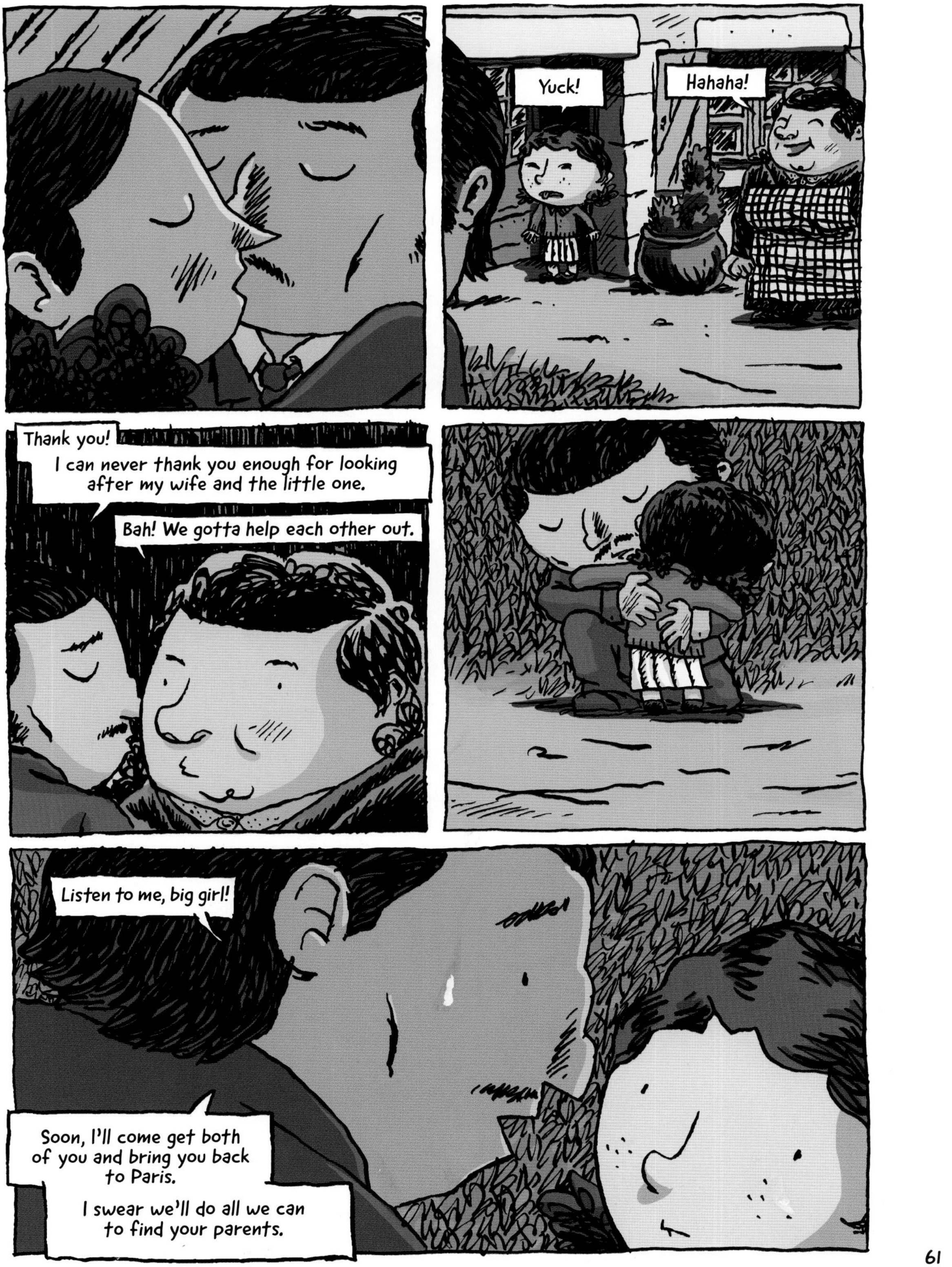
Yuck!
Hahaha!
Thank you!
I can never thank you enough for looking after my wife and the little one.
Bah! We gotta help each other out.
Listen to me, big girl!
Soon, I'll come get both of you and bring you back to Paris.
I swear we'll do all we can to find your parents.

A few months later, he did come to get us.

We were very sad to leave Germaine alone.

Luckily, her son came to live with her.

He had been in the Resistance, too.

And he didn't come home alone!

Emile kept his word.

He and Mama took turns searching for my parents.

Once, they let me come along.

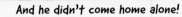

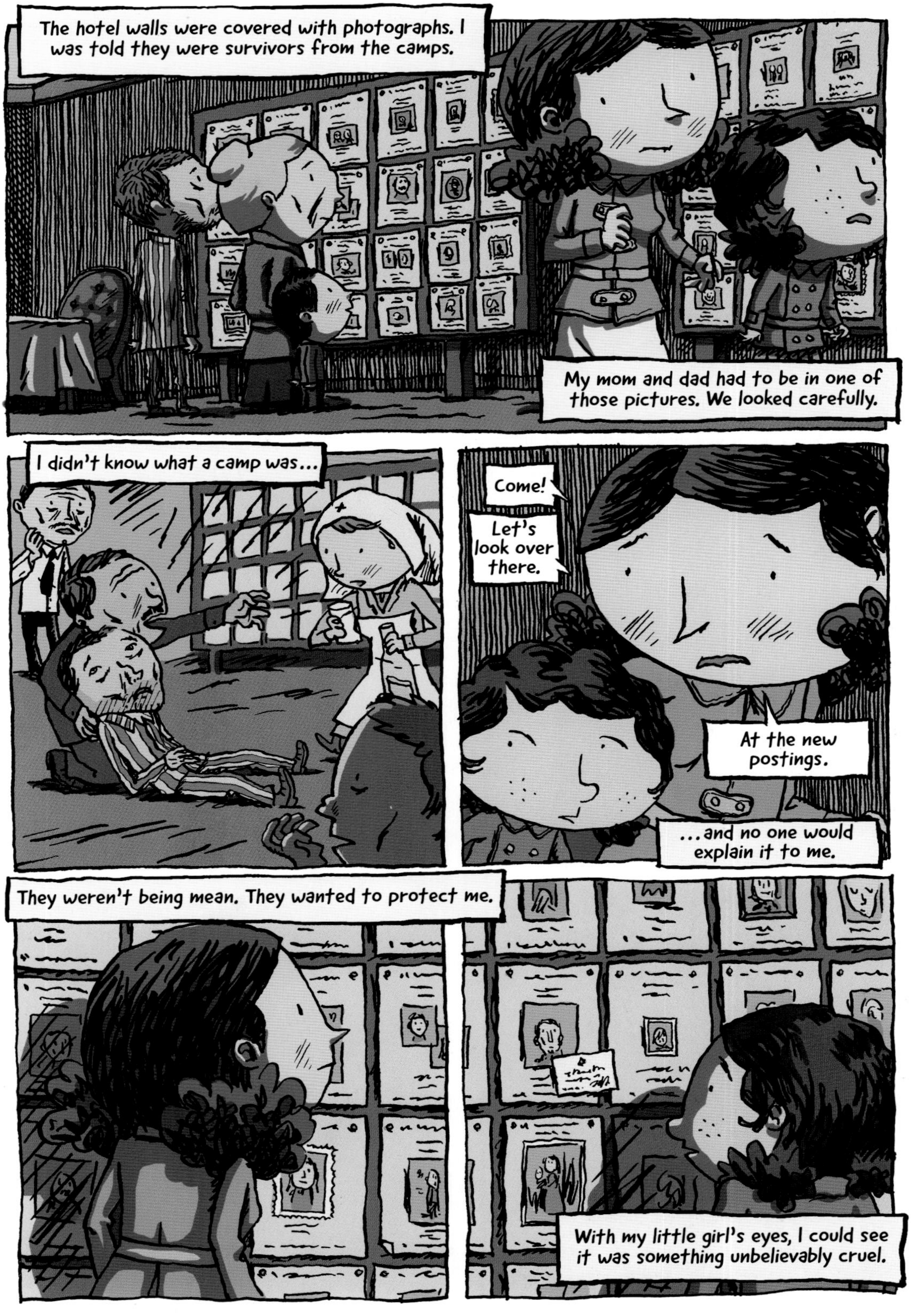
The hotel walls were covered with photographs. I was told they were survivors from the camps.
My mom and dad had to be in one of those pictures. We looked carefully.
I didn't know what a camp was...
Come!
Let's look over there.
At the new postings.
...and no one would explain it to me.
They weren't being mean. They wanted to protect me.
With my little girl's eyes, I could see it was something unbelievably cruel.

We made a mistake taking her there. We shouldn't have.

I don't think so. She had to see it. It's hard, but it will help her understand. Give her some time.

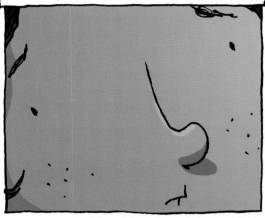

What will we tell her if we never find her parents?

We're not there yet. I'll go back every day if I have to.

Tomorrow, we'll have to sign her up for school. Can you take care of it?

Sure. You're right.

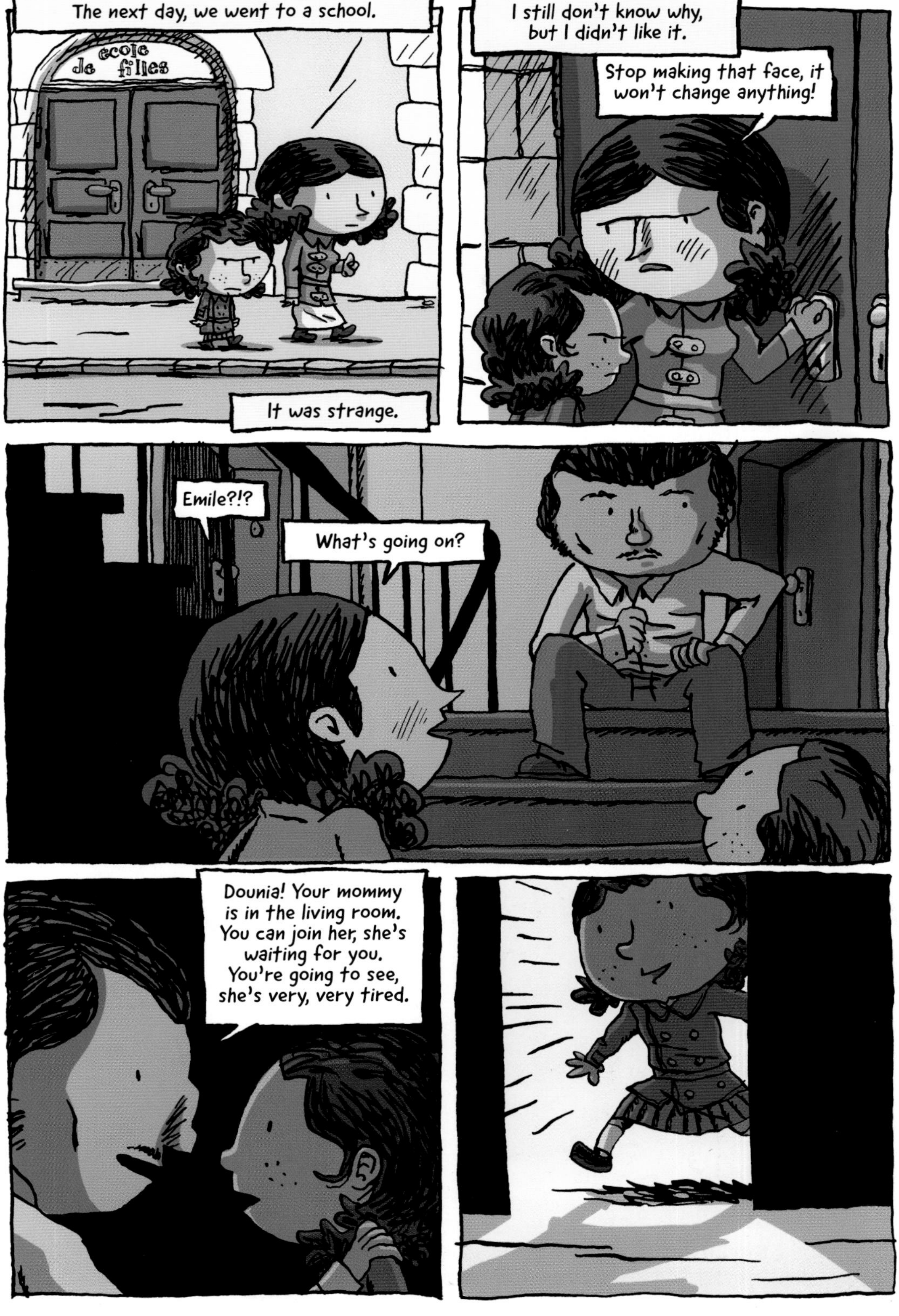
The next day, we went to a school.
ecole de filles
It was strange.
I still don't know why, but I didn't like it.
Stop making that face, it won't change anything!
Emile?!?
What's going on?
Dounia! Your mommy is in the living room. You can join her, she's waiting for you. You're going to see, she's very, very tired.

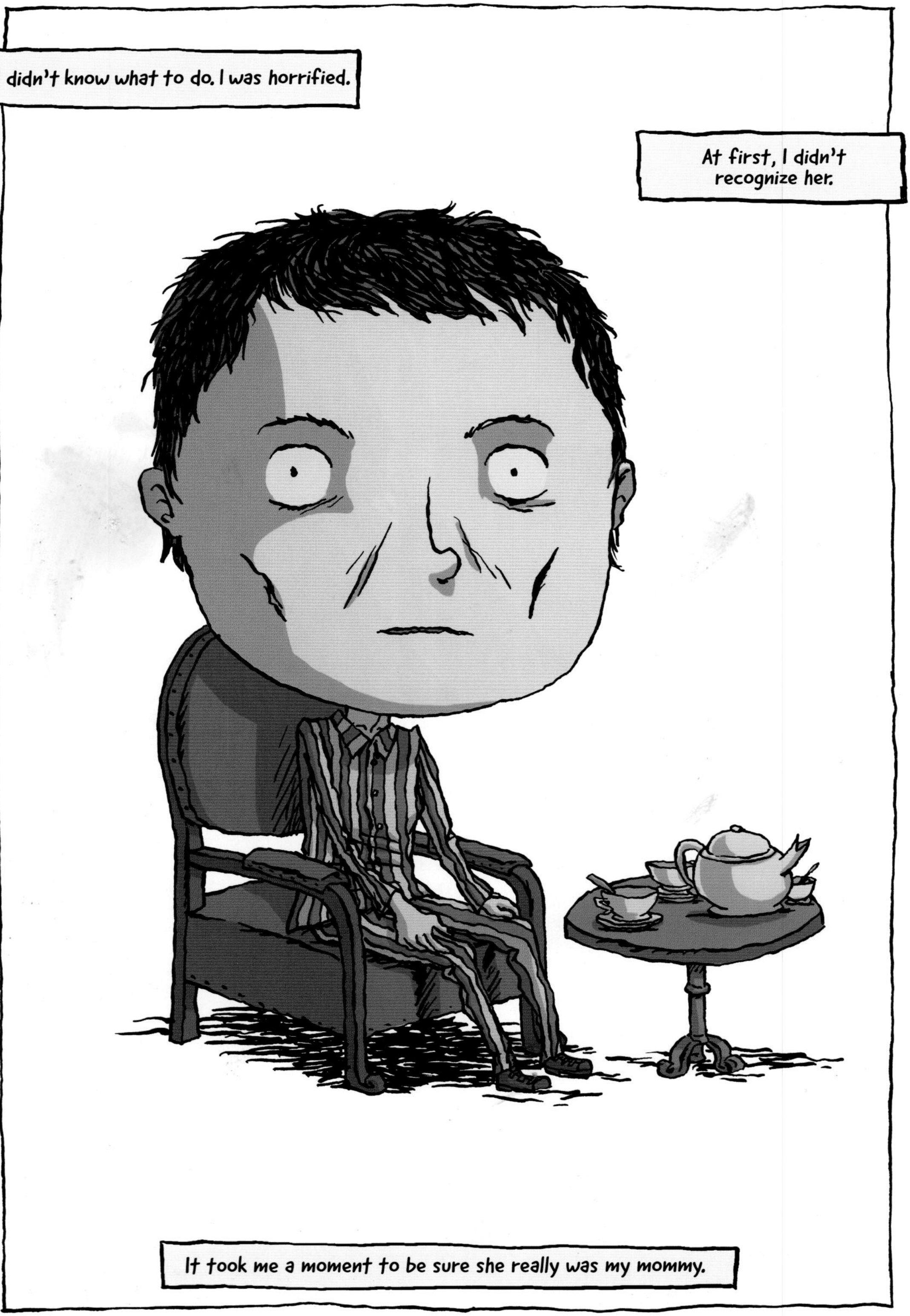
I didn't know what to do. I was horrified.
At first, I didn't recognize her.
It took me a moment to be sure she really was my mommy.

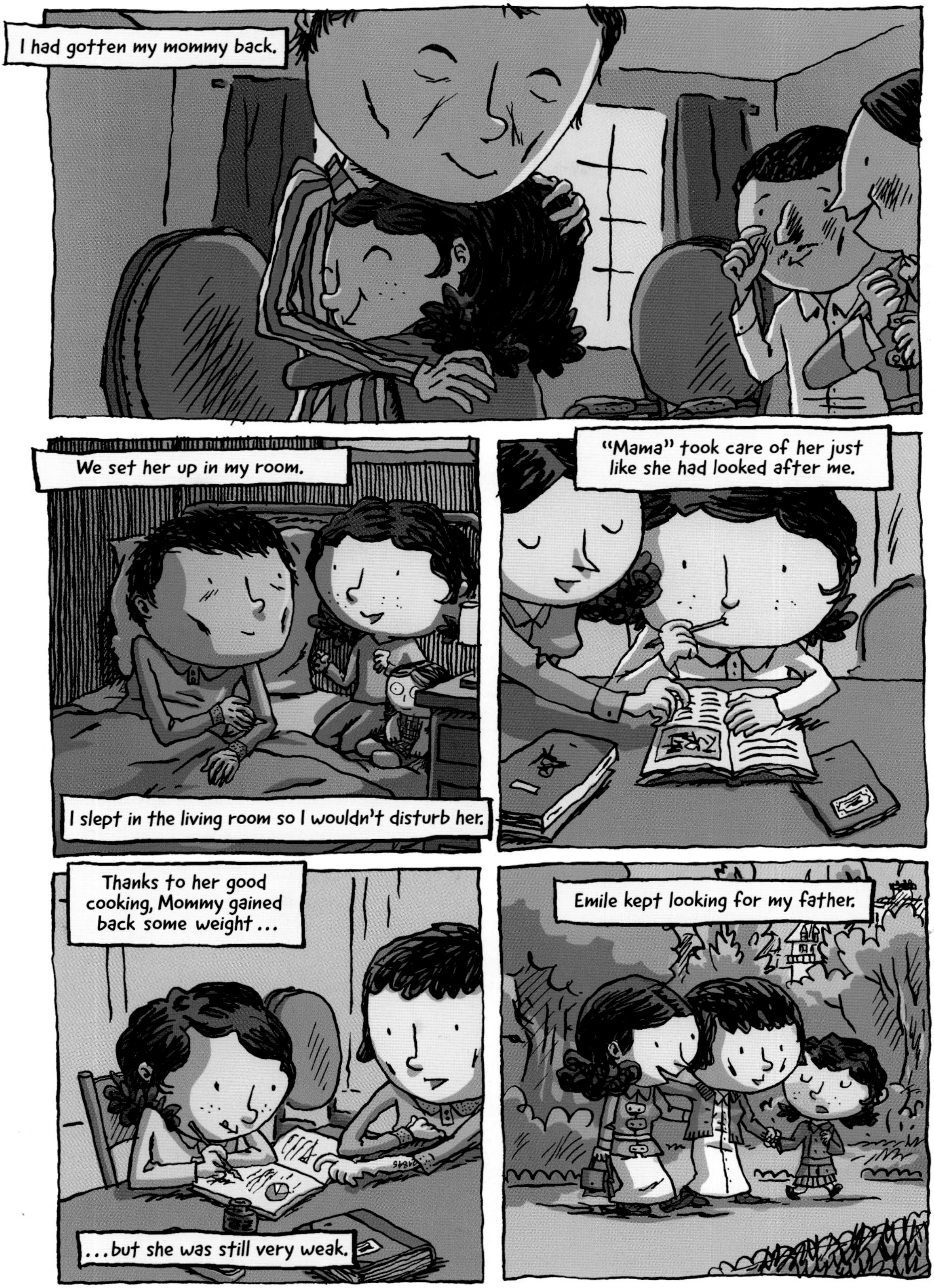
I had gotten my mommy back.
We set her up in my room.
I slept in the living room so I wouldn't disturb her.
"Mama" took care of her just like she had looked after me.
Thanks to her good cooking, Mommy gained back some weight . . .
. . . but she was still very weak.
Emile kept looking for my father.

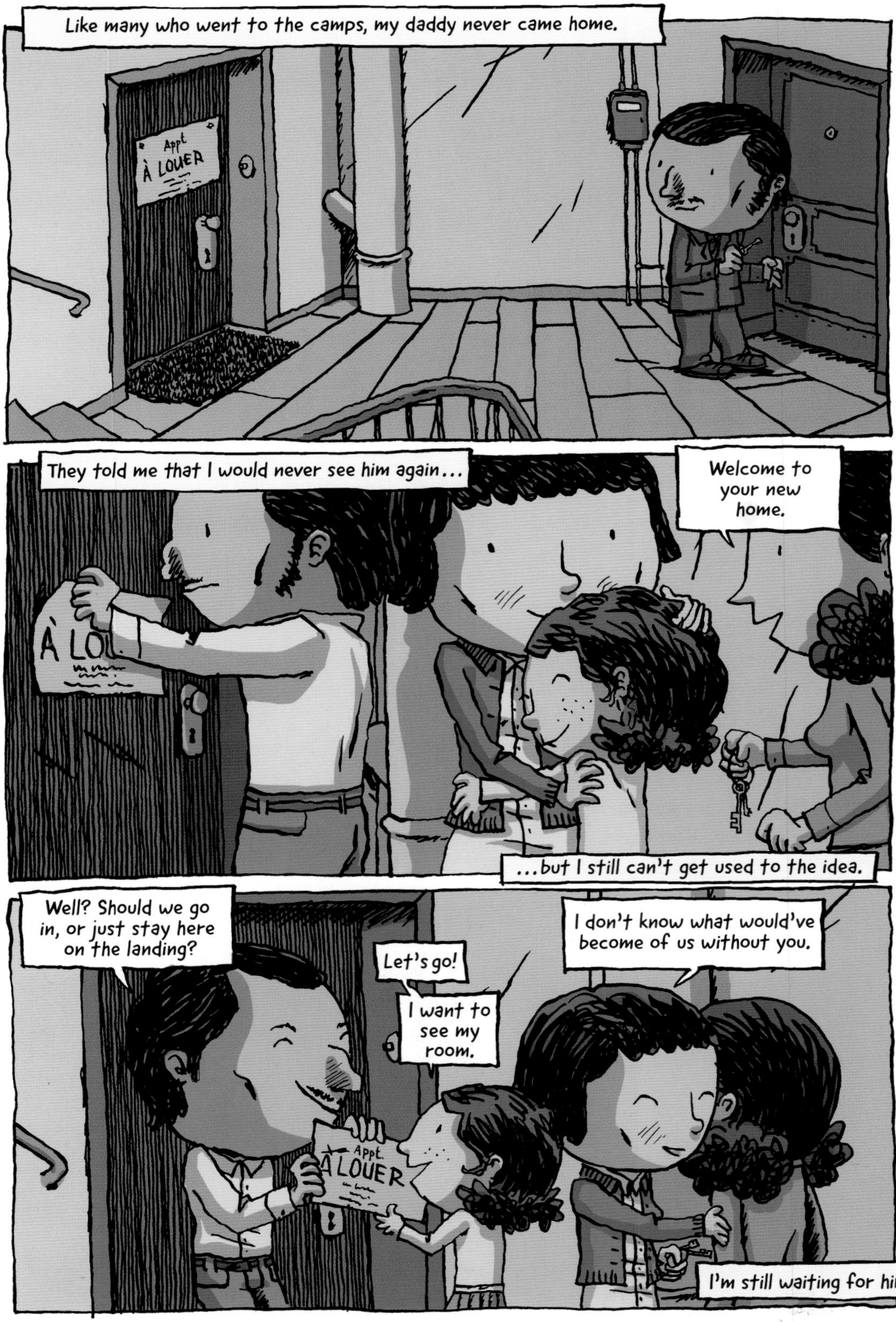
Like many who went to the camps, my daddy never came home.
Appt
À LOUER
They told me that I would never see him again...
Welcome to your new home.
À LO
...but I still can't get used to the idea.
Well? Should we go in, or just stay here on the landing?
Let's go!
I want to see my room.
I don't know what would've become of us without you.
Appt.
À LOUER
I'm still waiting for him.

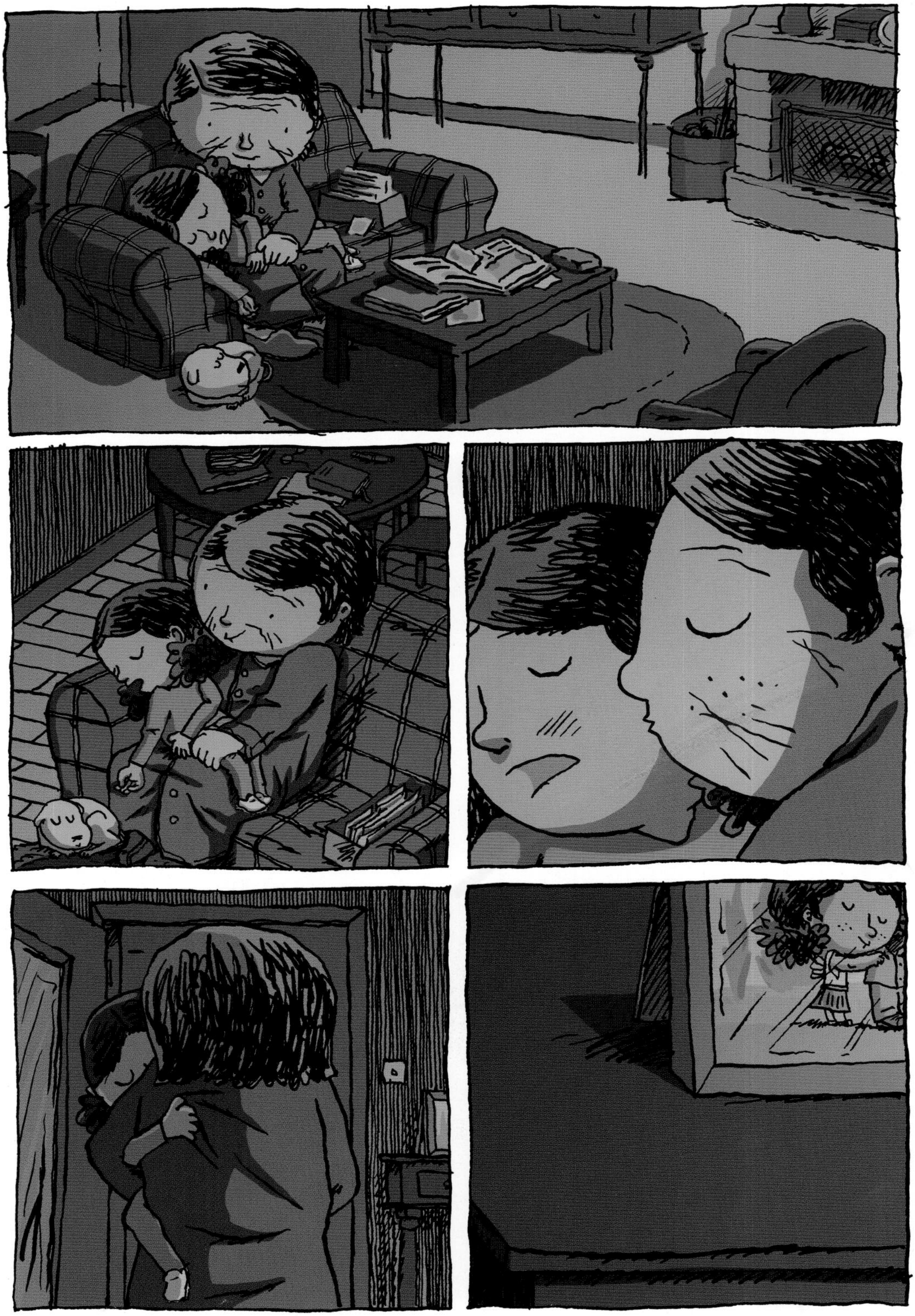

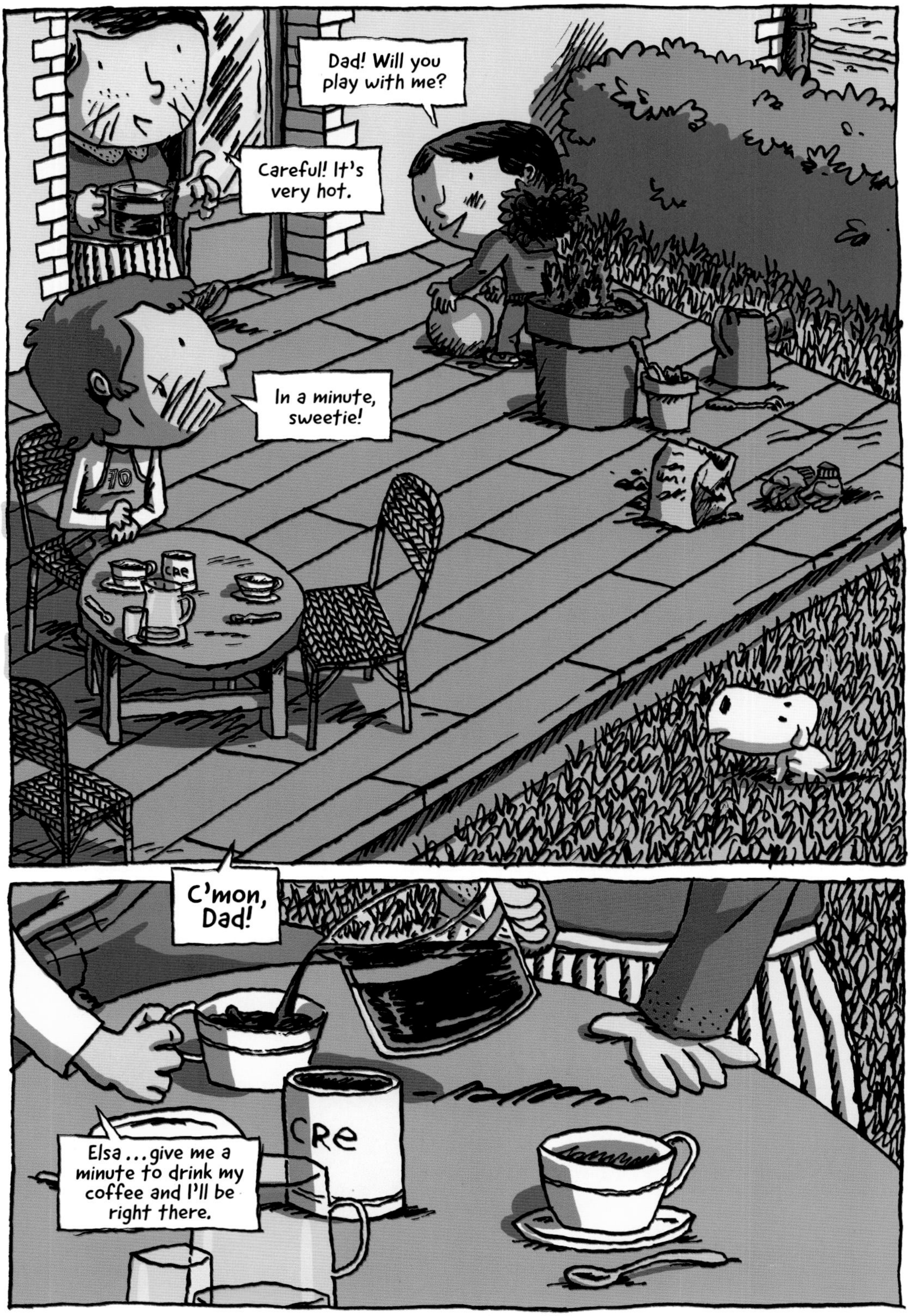
Dad! Will you play with me?
Careful! It's very hot.
In a minute, sweetie!
C'mon, Dad!
Elsa...give me a minute to drink my coffee and I'll be right there.

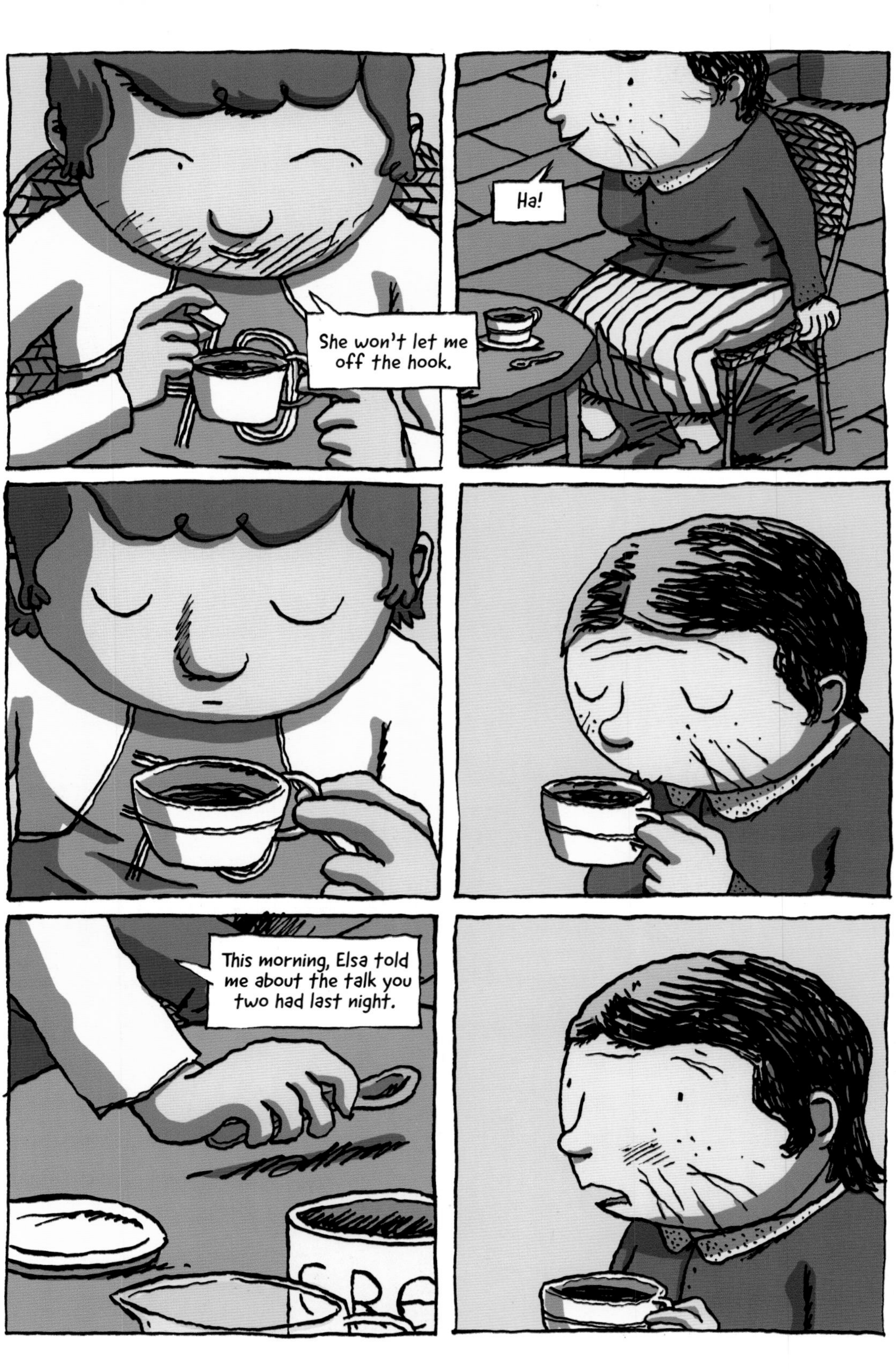
She won't let me off the hook.
Ha!
This morning, Elsa told me about the talk you two had last night.

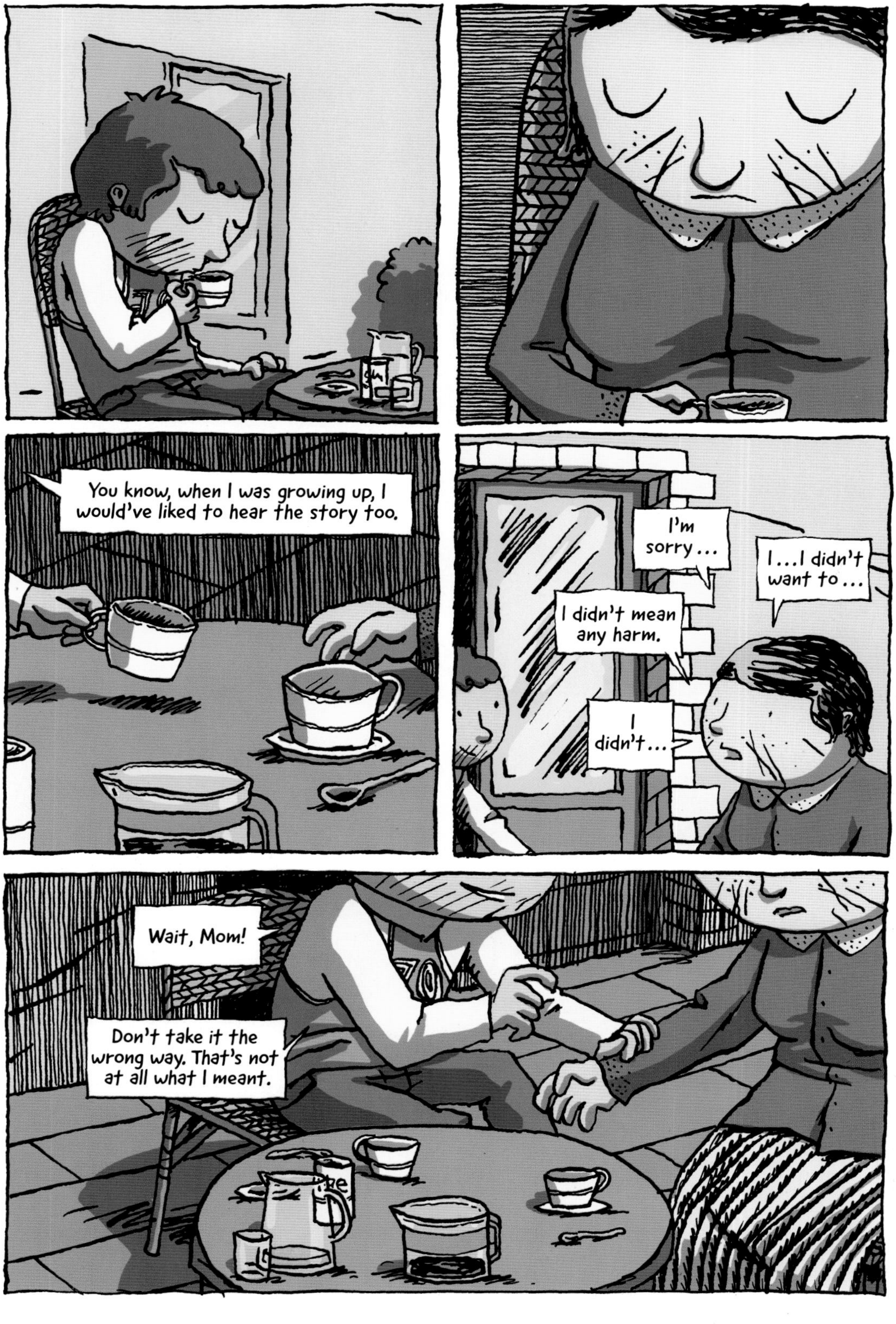
You know, when I was growing up, I would've liked to hear the story too.
I'm sorry...
I didn't mean any harm.
I...I didn't want to...
I didn't...
Wait, Mom!
Don't take it the wrong way. That's not at all what I meant.

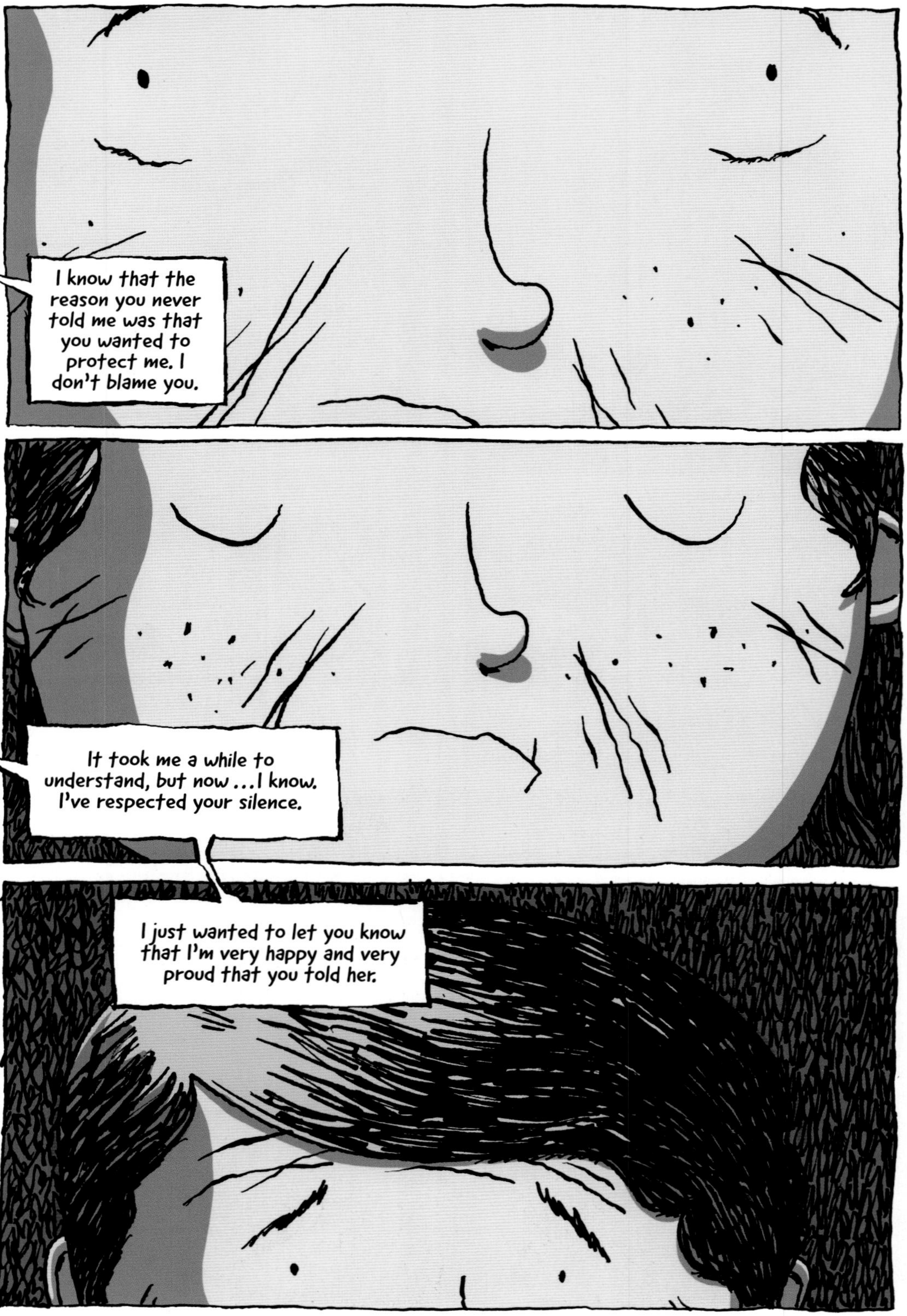
I know that the reason you never told me was that you wanted to protect me. I don't blame you.
It took me a while to understand, but now ... I know. I've respected your silence.
I just wanted to let you know that I'm very happy and very proud that you told her.

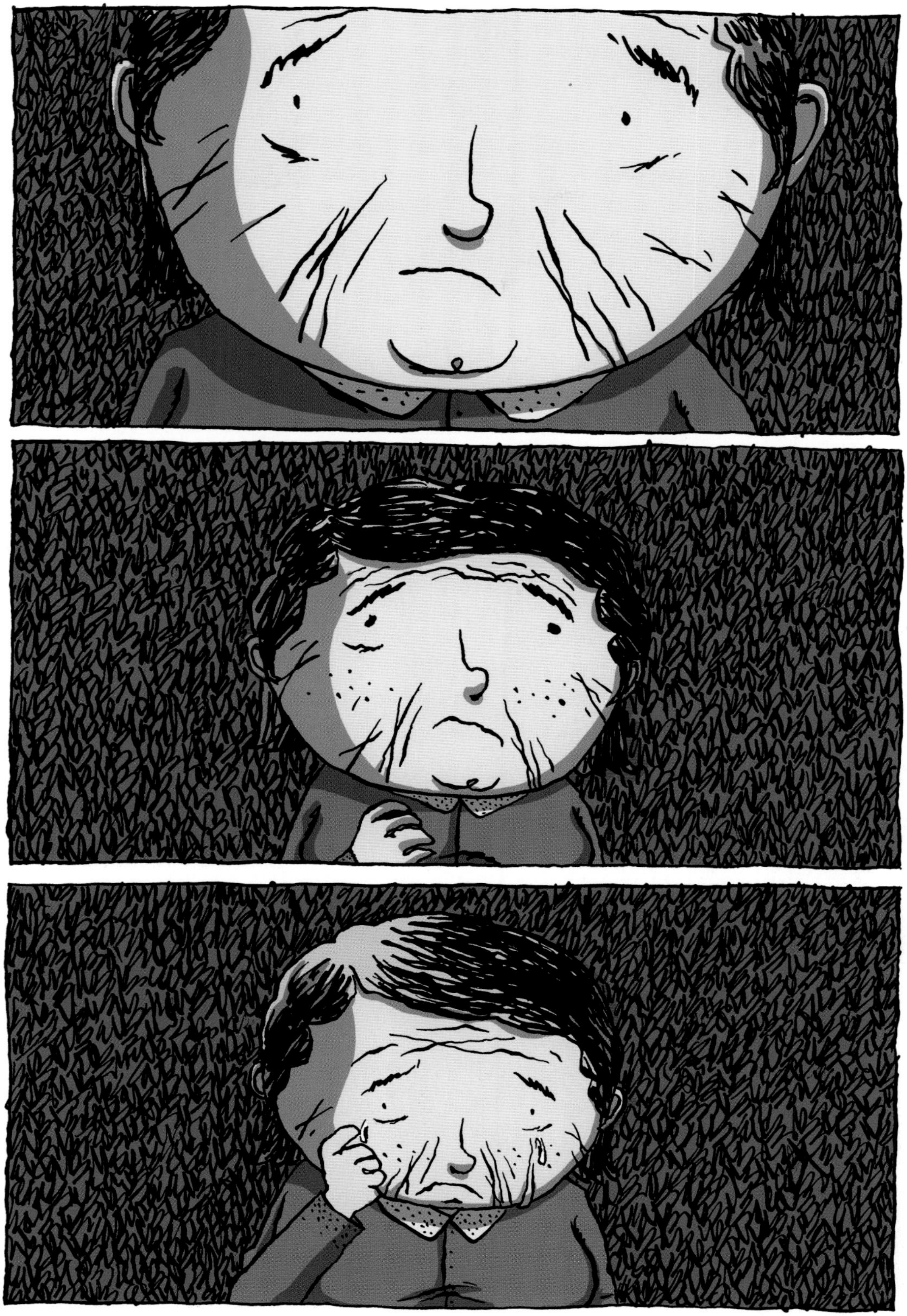

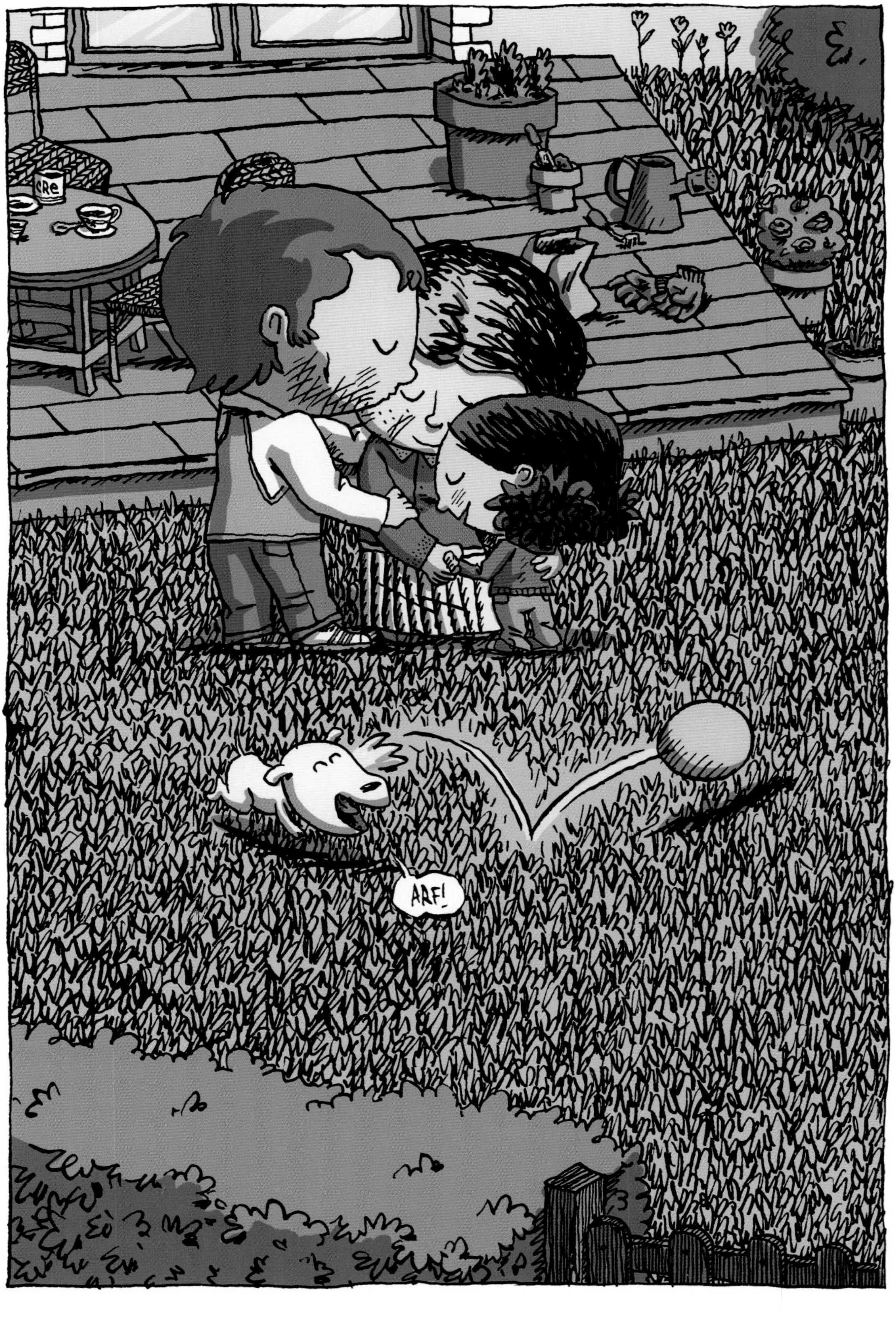
ARF!